COUNT DOWN

Count
DOWN

ADVENA ABDUCTIONS
BOOK ONE

HOLLIE HARTWRIGHT

PINDIKA PRESS
CANBERRA

Count Down (Advena Abductions Book One)

Published by Pindika Press
Canberra, Australia

Paperback 978-0-6488496-8-1

For my husband, who didn't bat an eyelid when he read this.

Author's Note

COUNT DOWN IS THE first short novel in the high-heat *Advena Abductions* science-fiction series. It is a fast burn, insta-connection, low-angst, super spicy MMMF alien romance with a HEA. Swords (and tentacles) will cross, and the lucky human heroine will not be choosing at the end.

Content warnings include a deceased family (in the past), an emotionally abusive ex (also in the past), references to mental illness, and references to endometriosis. There's also some space violence, and a mention of r*pe, trafficking, and forced breeding. There is explicit sexual content (all consensual), including M/F, M/M, and group scenes, and pregnancy. If you think I've missed something from this list, please, *please* contact me so I can update it. I am committed to keeping my readers safe.

Also, this is an alien romance, so, y'know ... There are alien *bits*.

This series is written by an Australian author, using Australian English. There's also a lot of swearing. These things may or may not be connected.

Terms and Definitions

Elyn: a being fated to bring harmony to a small, personal universe. The roles and understandings of *elyn* differ across cultures.

Elya: a fundamental energy force existing throughout the known universe, seen and channelled only by a rare few.

Biostamp: a collection of biological markers used to prove identification across the known universe.

Screencast: a video capture, either live or pre-recorded.

TESSA

The Advena Club lay off one of the city's busy main streets, tucked between an all-night café and a tiny second-hand book-shop. Its entry was a cherry-red door that was always closed, even when the club itself was open. A pair of muscled bouncers lurked behind it, looming under a neon-pink sign that blinked out the message *hic sumus omnes advena*: *we are all strangers here*. Once you showed your ID, they'd press a stamp shaped like a question mark on the back of your hand; the ink didn't come off for days.

It was one of those clubs that people just seemed to know about. I'd never seen so much as a flyer for advertising, and yet from Thursday through to Sunday from the hours of 9pm until dawn, Advena was packed with sweating bodies swaying to an eclectic soundtrack. The patrons were as diverse as the music: every subculture the city had to offer walked, wheeled, stumbled, or tottered on six-inch heels through Advena's bright red door. The dance floor was the place they all converged, the melting-pot of styles coming together under the ever-shifting strobe lights like a flock of gorgeous, mis-matched birds.

I wasn't part of any of their groups, and nor was I the kind of person who generally frequented trendy bars. I'd never really fit in anywhere, but I didn't feel like too much of an outsider at Advena. I'd tripped against its closed red door two years ago after a particularly bad dinner with my ex-boyfriend, mascara tracking down my cheeks and one of my heels snapped in half, crying and shaking as an unexpected storm dumped inches of freezing water on the city. Advena's chef, Anna, had been clocking on and had taken pity on me, letting me inside and giving me her blazer to cover up my soaking party dress. The bar manager, Maeve, had fixed me a gin and tonic so good it made me moan and so strong it made me forget some of the horrid things my boyfriend had said to me.

I didn't forget everything, though. The night I'd found Advena had been the last straw, and I'd finally found my backbone and broken up with him, moving out of the apartment we'd shared and into Maeve's larger one. Stumbling into Advena had given me a new place, a new job, and two new friends in the form of Maeve and Anna, and I'd done my best to forget the years of sustained emotional warfare my ex had put me through. I still didn't feel like I *fit*, but at least I was in charge of my life now.

But even two years later, some of the things he'd said that night still haunted me. *Not pretty enough, not smart enough, not thin enough, not funny enough. Try harder, Tessa, for fuck's sake. Nothing you do is ever enough.*

'Stop that,' Maeve snapped. She pushed a drink at me from across the bar.

'Stop what?' I said.

Maeve gave me her patented *I-don't-have-time-for-your-shit* glare, honed over years of dealing with drunk dickheads. Even though I saw it regularly, it wasn't normally aimed at *me*; I squirmed in my seat. 'I know exactly where your mind is,' she said. 'You get this look on your face like someone gave you decaf coffee whenever you're thinking about the past. Stop it. You're here for a reason. Drink up and start looking.'

The drink was blackcurrant gin and tonic; it smelled divine. Maeve added a wedge of lemon and a handful of blueberries poached from Anna's berry bowl; I leaned across the bar and grabbed some mint leaves from Maeve's carefully-arranged tray, dropping them in my drink. I took a sip, then sighed. 'Perfect.'

Maeve gave a smug smile as I settled back down and pulled at the hem of my dress. It was short, much shorter than I'd usually wear, and the inches of thigh exposed to the night and to other people's eyes made me uncomfortable. *You could never pull off a dress like that*, my ex taunted in my memory. I took another sip and pushed the words away with effort, concentrating on the music, which was some form of late-nineties House, with a pounding beat and relentless melody. The dance floor was full of writhing bodies, and the booths along the walls were similarly stuffed. The club smelled like sweat and summer and spilled rum.

Normally, I'd be wearing jeans and a shirt with my favourite heeled boots, and be sitting at the end of the bar with a drink in one hand and an e-reader in the other. But after months of Maeve trying to persuade me to find a hook up – or several of them – I'd finally agreed to come to the club to try, although our definitions of *hooking up* differed. Maeve insisted I needed some kind of sexfest; I was aiming for a dance and maybe – *maybe* – a kiss.

'What about him?' Maeve said, nodding her head to a pretty blonde with ice-blue eyes. He wore a polo shirt and chinos, but in an uncomfortable way – possibly because his mother might have picked them out for him.

'Please tell me you checked his ID before you served him.'

'There's a lot to be said for being the older woman, Tessa,' Maeve drawled, wiping down the bench.

'You'd know,' I said into my drink.

Her lips curled up.

Maeve was gorgeous, tall and toned, with rich chestnut hair that fell in soft waves halfway down her back and striking blue eyes so sharp they could cut. She was wearing skin-tight jeans and a black midriff top, baring some of her many tattoos. She was beautiful, scary as fuck, and fierce as a riled-up lioness, which all meant that she barely had to crook a finger and there'd be a line of people waiting to jump into her bed. Maeve liked the thrill of the new, which was a nice way of saying that you never saw the people she slept with twice, though often you'd see two – or even three – at once. She was also prone to sharing her exploits, often in unnecessary detail.

Her stories made some of the erotica I'd read look positively vanilla.

'Oh. There?' she said, gesturing with her chin towards a beautiful, brown-haired man laughing with a friend as he downed a craft beer.

'His suit looks like it costs more than my car.'

'That isn't hard, Tessa.'

'Leave her alone, Maeve,' Anna said mildly, appearing from the safety of her immaculate kitchen to place a snack plate of vegetarian nachos by my elbow. I mouthed a *thank you* and stuffed a chip in my mouth. 'Tessa will find someone when she's ready.'

'She *is* ready,' Maeve shot back. 'Have you *seen* her browser search history?'

'Fuck off,' I said, grinning. 'How much were your subscriptions last month?'

Anna bit her lip, trying not to laugh. The tiny blonde chef had an air of frailty about her, like she'd break if you looked at her the wrong way, but she was the strongest person I knew. Stronger than Maeve, even, and Maeve could have led a country if she'd been even the slightest bit inclined. 'She's clearly doing fine all by herself, then,' she said. 'She might not *need* a man.'

'No one *needs* a man.' Advena's bookkeeper, Claire, offered a crooked smile as she followed Anna from the kitchen. As usual, Claire was sketching on her tablet, even as she walked; I didn't understand how she managed it. 'They're all optional extras.'

I smiled at her as she snatched up an avocado-laden chip then disappeared into the office.

'She bought a new dress,' Maeve argued, gesturing to the midnight-black number I'd drooled over for weeks until it went on sale. 'She has to test it out. It's the rule.'

'She's not looking for a used car, Maeve. Tessa doesn't *have* to do anything. But if you *do*, Tessa,' the chef went on, 'make sure you're doing it for the right reasons. *Don't settle*. You deserve someone who makes your heart race.' She paused. 'Also, text me tomorrow if you find someone and tell me about it. I'm sick of living vicariously through Maeve.'

I blew her a kiss as she went back to the kitchen. Anna didn't date, didn't do hook ups, and had never had a partner in the two years I'd known her. Though I thought Anna was probably right and I should be picky about who I chose, there was no way

I was letting someone in enough to touch my heart. If it was going to be racing, it would be purely from exertion, not from any type of feeling.

I wouldn't be hurt again.

'She's right,' Maeve said, with uncharacteristic seriousness, echoing my thought.

'About what?' I sipped my drink and picked up another corn chip.

'Don't settle.' Maeve jabbed a stern finger in my direction. 'You deserve the fucking universe, Tessa. You've put yourself on the shelf for two years over some small-minded asshole who never deserved you. Make sure that whoever's attached to your new dick fits as well as your new dress.' She narrowed in on someone behind me. 'Oh. Him?'

Her eyes were on the dance floor, which could have meant she was looking at anyone. I turned around in my chair, trying to follow her gaze. I thought she was probably looking at the burly red-head who could pick me up one-handed and who had an endearingly crooked nose, possibly broken while running at speed towards other men wearing tiny shorts and wrestling over an inflated pig skin, but my eyes skimmed past him, drawn to the movements of someone else, someone obviously searching for a friend as he checked the phone in his hand with a frown. He was shorter than the red-head and far slimmer, but he had shoulders I wanted to trail my tongue over and the kind of forearms and hands that made heat sweep over my skin, strong and graceful, like he was an artist or a musician. His head was crowned in jet-black curls and I couldn't quite make out his features through the crowd, but he must have been wearing contacts, because when I glimpsed his eyes they caught the lights oddly, glowing molten gold.

I shivered and turned back to the bar as Maeve moved away to serve a woman wearing a floor-length sequined evening dress who was clearly going to or coming from somewhere *far* fancier than Advena.

My phone vibrated against my skin; I fished it out of my bra with a wince.

The text was from my cousin, Rian.

Nailed it ;)

I squealed out loud. Rian and his mother were my only living relatives. My aunt had moved back to Ireland years ago, but Rian had stayed living in his tiny flat in Melbourne. He'd just sat the detective exams and had clearly passed with flying colours. I sent an excited text in response with a load of exclamation marks and heart emojis, smiling proudly and promising to call him tomorrow. When I was done, I scrolled through my social media feeds.

At the age of twenty-seven, my social feeds were erratic: half my contacts were getting married and having babies, and the other half were still getting wasted at parties and ending up in different countries every fortnight. They were all *contacts* though, not friends. I'd connected with some people at university, but they were scattered across Australia now, and they weren't the kind of people I'd pour my heart out to. Over time – and somehow without me realising it – my world had narrowed to job I didn't like as the manager of a busy coffee shop, and to Maeve, Anna, and Claire, who had their own worlds and their own interests and who tolerated me good-naturedly as I clung to their metaphorical skirts.

Though I scrolled through social media a lot, I didn't post. It seemed too much like admitting failure.

'Tessa,' Maeve hissed. I looked up, startled, as she jerked her chin at the dance floor again. 'Someone likes your dress.'

I looked across, and got caught in the same pair of golden eyes.

'Did you change the lights?' I muttered, but I didn't spend too much time wondering; I had other things to stare at. The man had moved through the dance floor crush and I could see his face clearly. With golden skin, thick black brows, and cheekbones I'd kill for, he looked as if he should be pouting on the landing page of some high fashion website while someone equally attractive traced a finger along his perfect jawline.

Standing further away from the brick-wall-sized rugby player, it became immediately apparent that he wasn't small, either; I'd been misled by the sheer size of the other man. His lips curled up at the corners as I took in the black t-shirt straining over his shoulders and chest.

'He's probably looking at you,' I decided, turning back to my phone. People like that didn't look at me. Especially not while Maeve was in sight.

'Lean down and see where his eyes go,' Maeve said dryly. 'It isn't *me* he's drooling over.'

I wrinkled my nose, but bent down and pretended to fiddle with the zipper of my heeled boot, glancing back at the dance floor.

Maeve was right. Those glowing eyes tracked my movement, lingering on my thighs as my hem inched back up. Heat flared in my core at the hunger in his expression; no one had looked at me like that for – well, no one had *ever* looked at me like that.

'Go get him,' Maeve said. 'Before someone else does.'

I wavered.

'*Tessa*. At least go and see if he's as pretty close up as he is from far away.' She picked up a tray of dirty glasses and started walking to the kitchen. 'By the time I get back I want you on the dance floor. *With* that guy. One dance won't be life-changing. If he does anything you don't like, I'll eat him. *Go*.'

I bit my lip, waiting for Maeve to disappear. When she had gone, I checked my email instead.

'I suppose I'll have to work on my *come hither* stare.'

I looked up.

The man with the glowing eyes slid into the chair next to me, smiling slightly. Like a fool, I looked around, certain that he wasn't talking to me.

'Um,' I said, dazed, when his eyes stayed locked on my face and it became apparent that he very much *was*.

He was more beautiful than handsome up close, with gorgeously curved lips and a straight nose. His hair curled in gentle waves, like twists of the night itself. Sitting so close, his eyes were even more unreal; the contacts must have cost a fortune, because they really did seem to glow.

I bit my lip, hoping that my ovaries would calm down so my brain could begin to function again. 'Hi,' I managed.

He grinned, and my stupid heart gave a thump. *No way*, I told it sternly. *No way on Earth.* 'Hi,' he said, and held out a hand. 'I'm Aster.'

ASTER

THE SENSOR IN MY pocket was going wild, as if I hadn't already worked out that this was the human I was looking for. I ignored it. I didn't know how to turn it off anyway, and its signal would let Cy know that our hunt had ended.

It couldn't have *possibly* ended better.

The club was crowded, the humans constantly moving in a wave of heat and sound and colour, so it had taken me longer than it should have to realise where the sensor was pointing. Once it gestured in the direction of the bar, though, there was only one option; the moment my eyes had fallen on her, I'd *known*. The stars were singing a rapturous melody, the sound ringing through my ears, overpowering the awful racket the humans were listening to. The welcome weight of destiny settled over my shoulders; I wrapped it around me like an invisible blanket.

'Aster?' she repeated, staring at my outstretched hand. I liked the way my name sounded on her tongue, the sound low and sibilant. 'That means star, right?' She shook herself, then reached out to hesitantly squeeze my fingers, glancing at my eyes. 'Makes sense.'

My lips curled up; I gave her an expectant look, waiting for her name.

'Oh! Tessa,' she said once she realised, flustered.

I liked her flustered; a pink blush spread over her cheeks. 'Tessa,' I repeated. 'That means gatherer of the harvest, right?' I glanced at her purple drink, full of berries and lemon and mint, and her barely-touched plate of some kind of human food. *Nachos*, I remembered from one of the screencasts. 'Makes sense.'

She looked me over, a slight frown furrowing her brow. 'What are you, Aster? A web designer for a baby names page? A writer? No one knows that.'

I grinned, enjoying the way her blush deepened. *Morgan is going to lose his mind*. 'I know a lot of odd things.'

I'd had over two millennia to learn them, to be fair. But I'd probably save that particular fact for a little later.

'So my name is odd?' she said playfully.

My smile widened. 'I've never met a *Tessa* before.' Or a human, but she didn't need to know *that* right now, either.

Her lips twitched. 'What's the oddest thing you know?'

I searched for something that wouldn't send her running away screaming, and settled on something familiar to her. 'Did you know that there are more viruses on Earth than there are stars in the entire universe?'

'I did not know that.'

'Or that no one knows who named the Earth?'

She smiled. 'Are you a scientist?'

I did have several qualifications in various scientific disciplines, but she wouldn't have heard of most of them. *An astronomer, maybe.* I shook my head. 'Not really.'

'So tell me an odd fact that *isn't* about the Earth.'

I bit my bottom lip. I could tell her *infinite* facts about the universe outside her pretty little blue planet, but I settled on something Earth-related that I found interesting instead. 'Gustav Klimt lived with his mother his whole life.'

She blinked. 'Did you just tell me a weird art fact?'

Satisfaction thrilled through me, raising my temperature. I leaned away from her so she wouldn't notice, as if I was studying her. 'Do you want another one? Andy Warhol owned mummified feet.'

Tessa picked up her strange drink and took a hasty swallow.

'Oh, I think you liked that,' I purred. 'Here's another.' I shifted back closer, letting my scent wash over her. Her pupils dilated as it started to work, shifting her neural pathways so she could understand Morgan when he arrived. Being a living translator was a skill I was particularly grateful for; like a large number of species, Morgan's kind communicated via growls and snarls, and I wasn't sure Tessa's throat could manage the sounds. 'Michelangelo didn't bathe.'

Tessa gave an arch sniff, but her skin had broken out in gooseflesh. I resisted the urge to lean forward and trail my tongue over her bare shoulder. 'Everyone knows that one,' she said; it should have been disdainful, but it came out too breathy for scorn.

'Frida Kahlo lied about her birth year. Joy Hester had Hodgkin's disease.' I leaned closer, so close that my breath brushed her ear. 'Georgia O'Keeffe painted in her car.'

She shivered, shifting on her seat. I wanted to keep her warm and make her shiver all at once. 'Are you an artist?'

I sat back. 'I've done some metalwork. It's fun.'

'Where is your accent from?'

I repressed a smile; I'd picked it up watching five straight years of Earth screencasts, and it was a tapestry of mimicry. 'All over.'

'You're an adventurer, then.'

A woman with rich chestnut hair and many tattoos passed by behind the bar, giving Tessa a satisfied look. She mouthed something I didn't really catch; it looked like *new dress new dick*, but that couldn't have been right.

'An adventurer?' Yes, but not in the Earth sense. 'Maybe.'

'An explorer,' she said teasingly. 'A wayfarer. A wastrel. A flaneur. I bet you have a complex and mysterious backstory, and that you're only in the city for one night.'

My lips twitched. '*Wastrel*? *Flaneur*, maybe. An observer is close.' I paused. 'And I am only here for one night.'

Tessa's lips quirked up. 'And what do you watch, exactly, Aster the Observer?'

I gave a dangerous smile. 'The skies. The worlds. Right now, beautiful women. Well, *a* beautiful woman. Singular.'

She snorted into her drink. 'You just used your only free pass on corny lines.'

My smile widened. Tessa was *fun*. 'Good thing it was an excellent one, then.'

She sucked her bottom lip between her teeth. 'Where was the last place you were observing beautiful women? Or woman, singular?'

A planet further away than you could imagine, and not one being there compared to you. 'I'm not sure you would have heard of it. It's quite far away.' My eyes caught on her drink. 'What *is* that?'

'Blackcurrant gin,' she said, combining two words that made sense separately, but less when pushed together. I frowned. Perhaps I still had a lot to learn about humans.

She picked up the glass and offered it to me. I wasn't about to refuse something that had touched my *elyn*'s mouth, so I took a polite sip, then made a face as the taste rolled across my tongue. *Oh, no. Absolutely not.*

She blinked at me, and I realised that I'd muttered *humans* out loud. I grinned. 'And what do you do, Tessa, gatherer of the harvest? Other than have appalling taste in drinks?'

She took her gin back with a pout, cradling it like protectively. 'I serve coffee.'

I studied her face. The truth, but not all of it, if I was reading her properly. 'Yes?'

'*And* save up to go back to university.'

I settled into my chair. 'To go back and do what?'

'My Masters in Art History.'

My lips tugged up at the corners. 'So you *did* like the weird art facts.'

'Very much.' She considered her drink, seeming to think hard about something for a handful of moments before she drained the glass dry. I watched her throat as she swallowed, heat rolling over my body for another reason. 'Do you dance?' she said.

Interest stirred in my stomach. 'I've never really tried.'

'Would you like to?'

'Very much,' I echoed back to her, before I paused.

We were supposed to do this *together*. Morgan and Cy should have been here by my side as we met our *elyn*. We'd talked it through and agreed. We were a trio, a package deal – you couldn't have one of us without the others, and they were just as desperate to meet her as I was. I didn't want to give Tessa the wrong impression, and I didn't want to betray Morgan and Cy's trust.

'Aster?' she said softly, her green eyes wary.

But I also had non-existent impulse control, and Tessa looked good enough to eat.

I was *almost* certain that Morgan wouldn't try.

It was the wary expression in her eyes that won me over in the end, like she was waiting for a refusal. She was my *elyn*; I'd bring her every star in the sky if she asked for it. I'd never let her feel like I'd refuse her.

I gave her the smile that made Cy blush, and was gratified to see her cheeks go pink once more. 'You might have to lead me, starlight.'

Her blush deepened. 'If you get stuck, just stand still, and I'll move around you.'

My smiled widened. 'I'm sure I can manage that.'

TESSA

Perfect. This couldn't be more perfect.

I led him to the dance floor, my fingers linked through his. His skin was oddly warm, as if his hands had just been cradled around a hot mug of coffee, and I silently begged my palms not to get sweaty. Anna came out of the kitchen and blinked at me as I pulled him through the bar line, a slight smile tugging at her lips.

My smile was somewhat wider. How could it not be? He was handsome as sin, charming, he liked art enough to know weird facts about it – *and he was here for one night*. It was as if the universe had heard exactly what I needed and deposited him conveniently on the bar stool next to me.

Thanks, universe.

I was leading the way until we made it under the strobing lights; I found myself suddenly spun and pulled close, a strong forearm crossing my waist so that my back pressed against his chest.

It was the first time someone had held me tightly in years.

I *melted*.

'This is how you dance, isn't it?' he said into my ear, over the pounding bass. A shiver swept through me as his breath fanned my skin, my nipples peaking almost painfully against my bra.

'Um,' I answered breathlessly.

I couldn't answer; I couldn't *think*, not when he was so close, and not when he started *moving*, his hands dropping to my hips and heat seeping through my body at the contact. My hand came up over my shoulder to trace his jaw, my fingers mapping out the shell of his ear before burying themselves in his mop of curly black hair, as if they had a mind of their own.

To be fair, I was almost entirely certain that my uterus had complete control of my body at this point; it certainly wasn't my brain driving the show.

He ran his nose down my neck. 'You're gorgeous,' he breathed. He pinned me close, then rolled his hips.

That move should have been *illegal*. My body lit up like a fucking firework.

Part of it was not being touched for so long, but part of it was purely *him*. He seemed to know exactly where to put his hands – spanning them over my hips, my stomach, trailing his fingers over my collarbone – and exactly how to move, as if he was using his body to support every movement I made, keeping perfect time. If I raised my arms, his came with it, trailing his fingers over my skin. When I turned, his hands slid over the small of my back as my arms hooked around his neck, holding me close while still letting me move freely. And while Advena's dance floor was notoriously libertine, and there were couples and throuples all around us with hands in a number of interesting places, some of them openly trying to catch Aster's attention, his eyes stayed fixed solely on *me*.

And damned if that wasn't the best part of all.

He nuzzled behind my ear. 'Is this all right?'

'Mmm,' I managed.

He kissed down my neck; my knees went weak. 'You'll tell me if it isn't?'

'Mmm.'

'All right then.' His hand came up to cup my face, turning it towards him. He grinned down at me as I froze, mesmerised by his glowing eyes. 'Hello, starlight.'

For one impossibly long, tense moment, we stared at one another: me, as if I'd suddenly found God, and he as if I was a puzzle he very badly wanted to put together, then he dropped his face and brushed his lips over mine.

ASTER

BY THE FUCKING STARS.

I thought that after five straight years of research, I knew a little bit about humans. Their likes and dislikes, their customs, their clothing, their ways of speaking. But I wasn't prepared for the *taste* of her as Tessa's lips parted under mine. She was all sin and starlight, with a hint of the heinous blackcurrant nonsense; I ignored that cloying taste, sipping gently at her lips until all I could taste was *her*.

You should have waited, my brain chided.

Yes, I agreed, but my body didn't, tracing its tongue over Tessa's lip until she opened like a flower and brought her own out to play. My kind didn't have tongues in our natural form, and we were definitely missing out. When I nipped at her bottom lip, Tessa caught her breath, and it did all kinds of delicious things to me.

You're thinking with your dick again, my brain said, taking on Morgan's growling tones.

You're not here to stop me, I told it, *and if you don't show up soon, my cock is going to keep running the show.*

We've been waiting five years for this, my brain returned, in Cy's reasonable, measured voice this time, gently cajoling. *We should be together for it.*

My fingers tightened on Tessa's hips at that, because there was nothing in the universe that I hated more than disappointing Cy.

When Morgan's grandmother told us we had an *elyn* – a being fated to bring harmony to our world – I'd been skeptical, even when she provided a partial biostamp she'd seen in a dream. I wasn't one for faith – I was older than some religions, to start – but Cy took it as a challenge, and Morgan, for all his growling practicality, *was* a believer. When Cy decided to hack into the universal databases, I helped him, watching as the results came back from the hundreds of thousands of systems his big brain had breached, systems from all over, including from places we'd never even heard of and some systems that were very, *very* illegal. It was a risky move, but Cy knew what he was doing.

No one had been more surprised than me when the results came back with not just one match, but *three*. Three souls in the universe to whom that partial biostamp might have belonged; three souls in the universe who might be perfect for us, and us perfect for *them*.

We'd gone to the other two first, for no reason other than they'd been closer to Morgan's home planet of Natare. They had *definitely* not been our *elyn*. I hadn't expected the disappointment that had come with that realisation; the crushing feeling I'd had when I'd looked at them and their stars didn't sing.

Tessa's stars were singing to mine so loudly that I could barely hear anything else. They'd only sung like that twice before in my life: the day I met Morgan, and the day I met Cy.

I might not be religious, but I trusted the stars. I was made of one, after all.

I spanned my fingers across Tessa's waist.

You're old enough to control yourself, I knew Morgan would say. *Wait for us.* I was just pulling myself together enough to try, when Tessa's tongue trailed itself over my bottom lip.

Tongues trailing across my bottom lip was something I really, *really* loved.

Sorry, Mor, I thought, and cupped her cheek in my palm to hold her still while I devoured her mouth.

She pushed closer, her breasts pressing against my chest, my thigh dangerously close to slipping between hers. Tessa was a mouth-watering collection of curves wrapped in a night-black dress, and I wanted to map every single one with my hands and mouth. I pushed her mop of ashy-brown curls back from her face and had a sudden, vivid image of those curls wrapped loosely around my fingers while I bent her over the pilot's bench of our ship's control room and fucked her until she screamed my name. The bench would be the perfect height, and it would also annoy Morgan, which was my favourite hobby. Hopefully it would annoy him enough that he'd join in, which was my other favourite hobby. It would also drive Cy wild, which was my other *other* favourite hobby.

Aster, Cy's voice said warningly. *Don't go too far.*

Tessa gave a soft moan and my brain shorted.

Objectively, I knew that there were other humans in the room whose faces were more symmetrical than Tessa's. Symmetry was a standard mark of beauty across the universe, regardless of species, and there were others in the room whose mouths were full and even to Tessa's smaller rosebud lips, their cheekbones higher and sharper, their skin without her freckles, but my body didn't care about objectivity. *Perfect*, my chest was thrumming, suppressing its purr with effort. *Beautiful*, my hands were tingling, itching to touch every single part of her. *Lovely*, my skin was singing, wanting to feel her sliding against it. *Mine*, my mouth was demanding, as it claimed hers.

She huffed a surprised laugh as I dipped her backwards, holding her securely. The sound sent a shiver up my spine and a flush of heat to other places. I moved my mouth to her jaw. A blush spread over her cheeks, a dark pink in the club's neon lights.

Our elyn, my brain whispered, in my voice this time. *Ours, forever.*

That's more like it, brain.

I nuzzled at her neck, drinking in her floral scent. She was wearing perfume, something light and playful, but her natural scent was deeper, layered and complex. I let myself smile against her skin. Morgan was going to love it; his senses were far stronger than mine, and I was willing to wager my left hand that Tessa's scent would be everything his hunter's instincts had ever wanted.

He'd been worried when we'd realised our *elyn* might be human. As a Category-3 planet – *intergalactic contact probable in the future* – prolonged contact with Earth was currently forbidden, and information about humans wasn't available outside highly-protected government systems. That hadn't deterred Cy, of course; the information in intergalactic systems hadn't been enough for him, so he'd hooked the ship up to a number of Earth's satellites. After a while researching and watching Earth screencasts, we'd concluded that our potential *elyn* would probably want and need similar things to Cy himself, whose body was humanoid in form.

Tessa's breath caught as I left a trail of tiny bites down her neck, and I reflected that we were possibly – and luckily – right.

She let her head fall back, trusting me to hold her, and need burned its way through my body, heating my skin. I gently pulled her upright and spun her around until I could gain control and lower my temperature, sending a plea to the stars that she hadn't noticed.

She giggled as I took her waist in my hands again, marvelling at how tiny it was compared to the flare of her hips. I liked the way Tessa's form dipped and curved; most of the women on the Earth screencasts I'd watched had been different, all lean thinness. I'd mostly devoured things humans called *dramas* and *sitcoms*, though I'd watched a smattering of *thrillers* and *romance*, and their *documentaries* had proved invaluable. Their *horror* and *fantasy* confused me, as many of the creatures depicted were ones I'd met, and their *sci-fi* made me frown and laugh in turn. Humans had gotten some things spot on; others were wildly inaccurate.

I supposed they'd learn just *how* inaccurate in the future.

Tessa spun back to face me, running her fingers through my hair, another thing I liked very, very much.

Her eyes were heavy, and she couldn't quite catch her breath. I could hear her heartbeat thrumming under the beat of the awful music. I might not have met a human before, but I knew what all those things meant when Cy did them.

'Are you sure this is your first time dancing?' she said huskily.

I grinned. '*Dancing*, yes. Other things –' I leaned in and nipped her earlobe gently '– very definitely *not*.'

Tessa shivered, and my cock went from *interested* to *need her immediately* in one almost-painful heartbeat.

I was used to wearing a humanoid body. I'd worn one when I'd first arrived on Morgan's home planet, and it had become comfortable with time. In moments like this, though, I wanted to be in my trueform. I wanted to be able to encompass Tessa completely, to touch every inch of her skin at once. In my trueform, I'd be able to sense exactly where she wanted to be caressed, and be able to see the parts of her that were hotter than others. In this organic body, it was all guesswork.

She drew in a sharp breath as one of my hands wandered down her back to cup her rounded ass.

Well, it was *informed* guesswork.

'Do you ...' She trailed off and bit her lip.

Biting her lip was *my* job, so I spun her once more before drawing her into a deep kiss, soothing over the place she'd bitten with my tongue, enjoying the way she panted for breath. 'Do I what, starlight?'

'Do you want to come back to my place?' she blurted, blushing again.

I knew what *that* meant from the screencasts. *Yes*, every part of my body shouted.

Wait for Cy and Morgan, my brain protested. *You said you'd do this together.*

Tessa slid her hands under my shirt and my brain went silent. Her fingers wandered over my stomach to my hips, exploring, tracing the lines of muscle. Her skin was warm and smooth, and I wanted her to touch me *everywhere*. She sucked lightly on my tongue and it sent my thoughts into an immediate spiral as I imagined what that would feel like elsewhere on my body.

She broke away. 'Come home with me,' she whispered, looking slightly surprised at herself. 'If you're only here for one night, then spend some of it with me.' She stepped back from my embrace and tugged her dress down her thighs. She shot me a heated look, slipping between the other dancers – I'd forgotten they were there, and forgotten where we were – then headed for the club's red front door.

I was following her before I realised what I was doing. She held the club's door open for me; once we were outside, I took her by the waist and lowered my mouth back down to her neck, pressing her spine against my stomach. She arched back against me, tilting her head to the side to give me better access, holding out her arm to a four-wheeled vehicle – *car*, I reminded myself – parked directly outside the club.

I let her go. 'We're taking a *cab?*'

She blinked at me, no doubt wondering why I sounded so delighted. After watching all the Earth screencasts, I'd become slightly fixated on their transportation. Taking a cab was something I *really* wanted to do.

'We can walk if you want,' she said. 'But it will take a while.' Her eyes flickered downwards. 'I'd prefer to get home quickly.'

I flicked my eyes up at the stars when she turned away, silently begging them for help. *Cy, Morgan, hurry up. I'm about to do something stupid.* I followed her into the back of the cab, clearing my throat as I took one last, desperate look for them. I wasn't worried about them finding me – Cy could find my biostamp in the middle of a solar flare – but if they didn't show up within two minutes of my arriving at Tessa's place, I would not be held accountable for my actions.

Tessa gave the driver an address and we pulled away from the curb as I struggled to work my seat belt. The ones in our ship were different, so it took me a few tries. Tessa gave me an odd look, so I slid my hand over her knee and caressed her skin to distract her.

It worked.

Her knees fell slightly open in a silent invitation. My mouth watered. Morgan would have lost his mind by now; even I could scent her arousal. My cock pressed painfully against my jeans, trapped somewhere it didn't want to be. I could have willed the proof away, but Tessa's eyes slid down again, and I wanted her to know how much she was affecting me.

I shifted across the seat and seized her mouth again, slipping my tongue between her lips in a slow thrusting motion I wanted to repeat elsewhere with my hips.

I waited for my brain to interject, but apparently it was done.

When the cab driver coughed pointedly a few minutes later, I raised my head, dazed.

'Oh, God. Sorry,' Tessa said, flushing, and fumbled inside her bra, fishing out a small plastic rectangle, which she held against a machine in the middle of the console. I took some notes from my pocket – Cy had managed to hack the generator to replicate some different forms of Earth currency – but Tessa waved it away.

I unclipped myself – the seatbelt was easier to *un*do, it turned out – and followed Tessa outside, realising I'd missed my first and only chance to experience a cab because I'd been ravaging Tessa's mouth. I tried to feel sorry about it as the car drove away, but Tessa took my hand and pulled me towards the front of a large apartment building, and I felt nothing but anticipation.

And lust. A whole lot of that.

Tessa led me inside a glassed foyer, then to an elevator. It opened immediately, and once the door closed behind us, her hands were back inside my shirt, roaming freely over my chest as she stood on the tips of her toes to kiss my neck. She was delightfully small, even though she was wearing boots with a heel longer than my fingers. I locked my arms around her – half to help, and half to keep her in place – and trailed my lips over the shell of her ear, revelling in the way she shivered.

The elevator stopped all too soon – or took much too long, depending on the way you looked at it – and Tessa drew me down a carpeted corridor and past several red doors, before she paused before one with the number *14* made out in gold numbers. She fished another plastic rectangle from her bra – I stared at her in admiration, wondering exactly how much she could fit down there – and she held it to the door until it beeped and let us in.

The apartment was simply but elegantly furnished; I recognised the style from a screencast I'd watched, set half a century or so in Earth's past. There were mint-green couches and bookshelves made of pine, and a tall lamp with a mosaic glass shade in a pattern of dragonflies.

There were two scents: Tessa's soft, comforting floral, and another that was muskier, heavier and assertive. I had no doubt that scent would drive other beings mad, but it wasn't for me. Tessa was pulling off her boots, revealing more of her silken skin, and then her tiny feet. I don't know if it was the feet that did it – how could they possibly be so small? – but my brain kicked back into gear.

This has to work, it asserted. *She has to come with us.*

Tessa stared at me, her green eyes heavy with want, and I completely agreed.

I took her waist in my hands and her mouth with mine, and I steered her towards the couch, spinning us around at the last moment so that when I sank back she came with me, straddling my lap. Her lips were demanding now, their soft yielding changed to passionate domineering; I let her lead, groaning as she took my face in her hands. Mine slid up her thighs and around to cup her ass, then moved higher to tug the tiny zipper down her back. She stood back up to shimmy her dress down her body; my mouth went dry when her bra and underwear followed it, and I was left with a gorgeous, naked, and very aroused human.

A female body presented a new challenge, but thanks to Cy's determined research, I had at least some idea of the way it worked. Anatomy charts were one thing, but seeing Tessa's curves first-hand was another. I could sense the heat pouring off her, see her shudder as she inhaled, smell her perfume and her arousal.

Which was exactly why I'd also watched a number of fairly explicit screencasts. Some seemed ludicrous, but others were more useful. Cy warned me to be careful with what I picked, noting that humans were not a gender-equal species, and that much of their media was skewed towards the male perspective and desires; Morgan, who came from an overwhelmingly matriarchal planet, growled at that.

Just listen to her, he'd said. *And pay attention. Like you did to me.*

I took Tessa's waist in my hands and drew her forward, trailing my mouth across her rounded stomach.

When I'd met Morgan – the equivalent of eleven Earth years ago now – I'd had to learn what he liked with no context. I'd had no prior experience of corporeal beings, let alone humanoid ones. Luckily, Morgan wasn't backward in coming forwards, and he happily showed me. Often. We barely left his bedroom for the first year. There were things we had to navigate – his urge to hunt in the water, for instance, and my non-corporeal trueform – but there was one thing that stood me in good stead: go slow and explore. It helped us both when we met Cy, whose body was different again.

Tessa was on a whole different level.

I nuzzled at the apex of her thighs, breathing in deeply. Her hands shot to my hair, bunching it between her fingers. She didn't pull me away, so I kept nuzzling, then trailed my hands up her thighs so my fingers could explore.

Her upper thighs were slick with arousal. I trailed my fingertips through it, pleased, then moved them higher, tracing where she was swollen. She was drenched and impossibly hot, and I was drawn to her heat like a magnet. I flicked my tongue out to taste her.

And moaned.

If her mouth tasted of sin and starlight, then her core was utter bliss. I indulged myself for a moment, working her with long, leisurely strokes of my tongue until her thighs trembled. I swapped our places, nestling her gently back on the couch cushions, and knelt between her legs, turning my attention to the swollen bud at the apex of her sex. Her body bowed and she threw her head back, whimpering; I slid my hands under her ass and encouraged her to move as she wanted, purring wordlessly when she pushed her hips up.

If I had more time, I would have made her show me what she liked. I would have watched her long fingers move over her own flesh, watched where she lingered, how she moved, observed the pressure she used and the speed of her fingertips. As it was, she was dripping onto the couch and arching, so I guessed that what I was doing with my tongue was passable, at least. I flattened it on her bud – her *clit*, the screencast had called it – and kept up a steady, relentless rhythm, trying to forget that the count down on my time here had already begun when I wanted to stay between her thighs until the stars burned out.

I was rewarded a minute later when she tensed; her body throbbed and she moaned my name, her hips pushing up. My mouth flooded with wet heat and I gave a moan of my own as my cock twitched against my jeans. She shuddered and shivered, writhing beneath me until I slowed, sucking gently before moving to clean her thighs with my tongue.

'Oh,' she said dreamily. 'That was ... mmm.'

I decided to take incoherence as a compliment.

She shook herself; a moment later, her heavy-eyed smile turned wicked. 'Your turn,' she said.

Wait, my brain begged desperately.

But how could I possibly say no?

TESSA

Who are you, and what have you done with Tessa? I imagined Maeve teasing. *Also, you're paying for deep-cleaning the lounge.*

It would need it.

I wasn't used to doing things like this, but somehow, the very fact I wasn't used to it made it easier. That he wouldn't be in the same city as me in twenty-four hours made it even better. I could be unapologetically myself, knowing that it didn't matter what he thought, or whether he liked me as a person. I could ask for what I wanted without feeling self-conscious – and *get* it.

I was tempted to let him stay exactly where he was. He didn't look inclined to move his face from between my thighs – which gave him infinite brownie points – but when he disappeared in a few hours' time I wanted to *know* exactly how I'd spent the night. Maeve was the adventurous one in our apartment; I was too self-conscious to fuck with the lights on, and I'd never done it on a couch before, but something about Aster made me relaxed, confident, and more than a little thirsty. I'd never wanted anyone so badly.

Couch sex it is.

I shifted so I was lying down properly and pulled him on top of me. My body was still shuddering; my limbs were heavy with pleasure and the neat straightener waves I'd spent an hour on were spiralling into my natural curls from the sweat at my temples. I didn't think I'd ever come so hard, and certainly not on someone's mouth. I would have felt embarrassed, except Aster had been so clearly into it; he'd made a pleased purring sound the whole time, the vibration making my clit tingle.

His mouth crashed back onto mine and I tasted myself on his tongue. I undid his belt and slipped my hand inside.

And almost purred myself.

He was long and thick and rock-hard, his head swollen and leaking precum. Like the rest of his body, his skin seemed hotter than normal, as if he'd just come from a bath or the gym. I hadn't done this in a long time, but I hadn't forgotten how; I worked him up and down with my hand as he kicked his jeans off, listening to him purr against my lips.

Maeve kept condoms in a card holder on the coffee table as a joke – she refilled them fairly frequently, so it wasn't all funny – and I reached back to grab one, tearing open the packet then rolling one over Aster's length. When I was done, he dragged his head over my slit, collecting moisture, before touching me gently with his fingers, slipping them inside me as if testing the waters.

His fingers crooked, and he pressed gently against the front of my inner wall, finding the sweet spot inside me with unnerving accuracy.

I bowed upwards, whimpering. He slipped his fingers out, but replaced them a moment later with the head of his cock, moving with small, gentle thrusts and giving me time to adjust as he worked himself inside me. He gave a deep, guttural groan when he bottomed out, and for a handful of moments he lay still, supporting his weight on his hands, his forehead resting on mine.

Then he began to move, and I forgot who I was.

He pulled back until he could angle his thrusts up, each movement hitting exactly where it felt best. Warmth and pleasure spread through my core, relaxing my muscles and sending tingles up my spine. I'd never felt anything like it; I let my arms fall back beside my head, giving myself over to his thrusts completely as my fingers found a cushion to twist.

'You are the heavens themselves,' he groaned.

I didn't think I could speak, so I pushed my hips up to meet his thrusts instead, grinding against his pelvic bone. He quickened his pace but kept his movements shallow, and soon enough I could feel pleasure building again, my core quivering.

'Tessa,' he ground out, as I started to clench around him.

The waves of pleasure broke and my body gripped him like a vice. He ran a hand up my thigh and pushed my knee back, sinking as deep as he could and thrusting hard. I shrieked as he fucked me through the last throes of my orgasm, my body milking him as the heat in my core intensified.

'Aster,' I whispered.

He kissed me, nipping my bottom lip, gasping into my mouth. His free hand came up and he twined his fingers through mine, his other hand tightening on my thigh as his thrusts quickened.

'Starlight,' he panted, and I felt his cock thicken.

'*Yes,*' I hissed. The heat inside me became almost unbearable. His spine stiffened and his back arched.

Then he disappeared.

I lay still for a moment, my heart beating in my ears as I stared at the place a man had been.

What the fuck.

I shrieked, scrabbling back on the couch. I was panting, empty and throbbing, my body still clamping down on something that was no longer there, and I was damp with sweat – *and not just my own*. Aster was nowhere to be seen, even though I could still smell his delicious spice on my skin. 'What the *fuck*?' I whimpered, my fingers twitching; just a moment ago they'd been intertwined with his. 'What the actual *fuck*?'

To make matters worse, there was a noise at the door, a slight scuffle of feet as someone outside it searched for a key. I grabbed wildly at the throw on the back of the couch, instinctively pulling it around my body so Maeve wouldn't get an eyeful. The lock beeped and the door pushed open just as I covered myself up.

Except it wasn't Maeve who stepped into our lounge room. It was a handsome blonde with muscles on his muscles, so tall his head brushed the doorway, accompanied by a slender, red-haired beauty with steel-grey eyes.

The blonde rubbed his temples with long, strong fingers. 'Seas below, Aster,' he said, in a low rumble of a voice. 'I knew you'd fuck this up.'

MORGAN

Aster was on the ceiling, floating in the pulsing darklight of his trueform. His glowing eyes were closed, possibly in embarrassment, though I knew it would be all too fleeting; Aster didn't really do *shame*. I raked my eyes over him, searching for the bleeding whitelight that meant injury, but there was nothing; beside me, Cy was running his own scans. He breathed a sigh of relief, which I took to mean our starling was unharmed.

My eyes flickered to the female on the couch.

She was scrambling to cover her nakedness with a grey blanket, pulling it this way and that, but it barely contained the parts she wanted to conceal.

My mouth watered as her scent hit my tongue. Floral, but it was more than that – she smelled like sea lilies. I imagined that her scent was normally lighter, but her evident arousal made it cloying, as if it was wrapping itself around my body and my brain and painting itself across my tongue.

Sea lilies were my favourite flower.

Cy looked her over, much less lecherously than I'd managed. 'Her heart rate is too high,' he said. 'Her pupils are dilated, and her breath is swift. She's sweating.' He turned to me. 'She's afraid.'

'You fucking *think*?' the female shrieked. 'Get the fuck *out*.' She clutched the blanket tighter; it merely highlighted her delicious curves and made my cock twitch. 'And where the *fuck* is Aster?' she muttered.

'Above you,' Cy answered, before I could stop him.

She tipped her head back, and took in what was floating near her ceiling.

She whimpered.

Aster's eyes opened and he blinked back at her, his irises glowing golden in the mass of floating darklight.

She scrabbled to the end of the couch, clutching the precarious blanket. 'What the *fuck*,' she whispered.

'Two millennia old and he still can't hold his corporeal form when he comes,' I said lightly, trying to distract her. 'It's annoying as fuck if you want to cuddle.'

Aster glowed darkly, then swirled downwards, back into his humanoid form, completely naked. 'Fuck you, Mor,' he said mildly. He crossed the room to Cy, tipping our love's head back to give him a thorough kiss. 'Where have you been?'

'It took us a while to find what we needed,' Cy said, his breath slightly unsteady after Aster's swabbing kiss. He curled a hand around the starling's bare hip. 'We had to try a few different places.' He glanced at the female. 'Apparently you didn't.'

Aster's skin gave off the golden glow it couldn't contain when he was happy.

'Shark-fucker,' I grumbled half-heartedly, knowing all too well Aster's habit of thinking with his dick rather than his brain. 'We were supposed to meet her together.'

'I tried, Morgan, but *look* at her. Perfect, isn't she?' Aster's voice rang with satisfaction. 'Our *elyn*.'

'I'm not your *anything*,' the female snapped, her cheeks a delicious shade of outraged pink. 'Aster, get your friends out of my apartment. Then you can get out, too. I don't know what the fuck just happened, but I did *not* like it and I am *extremely* pissed that I wasted a new dress on this.' She stood up and adjusted herself with the poise of a queen; Cy swallowed audibly while I laughed under my breath as her sea lily scent coated my throat.

Aster held up his hands, placating. The asshole was always magnificent, and he managed to be more so naked. The female was clearly not unaffected, her pupils blowing out as she took him in.

'Let me explain, Tessa,' he said calmly. 'Please.'

Tessa. I let the name roll over my tongue. Aster said it like a caress, but I liked the way it started with a short, sharp sound, then ended like a sigh.

She lifted her chin. 'You have two sentences,' she snarled, her eyes furious. 'Two *short* sentences. Then, if you're not gone, I'll call the police. Or worse, *Maeve*. She's been saying for years that she'd bite the cock off the next man to hurt me.'

I watched Aster consider her words. He was clever, my mate, clever and quick-witted and sharp, though the current circumstances might have suggested otherwise. I should have been angrier that he'd left without me and Cy – we did things together, and we always had – but because he'd left with our *elyn*, the fury wouldn't come. I was only slightly jealous that she'd fucked him first, but as I searched my feelings I realised that it came mostly from concern that he'd done things properly, though I shouldn't have worried. The female's eyes were bright and heavy, so Aster had clearly done *something* right.

Aster dissolved back into his trueform, keeping a vaguely humanoid outline this time, floating in front of the female like he'd dragged a piece of starlit sky into her apartment. *We're not human, and we've travelled for five years straight to find you*, he said, his voice echoing around our minds. Tessa blinked, then winced. It was hard to get used to, even more so when you weren't expecting it. *Please don't throw us out, Tessa.*

She stared at him, then rubbed her eyes. 'What the *fuck* did Maeve put in that gin?' she muttered.

Through some unexpected miracle, Tessa decided she wouldn't throw us out immediately. She'd poked at Aster's trueform and watched her finger disappear into the darklight before sinking back on the couch with her head in her hands, and I thought she was about to break down, but then she finally saw Cy properly and that seemed to distract her from her oncoming existential crisis. I couldn't blame her; Cy had a humanoid trueform just like hers, and an astonishingly beautiful one at that, with high cheekbones, wide grey eyes, and plush, infinitely kissable lips. I'd wanted him the second I'd lain eyes on him, so I couldn't exactly blame her for the same thing. She'd stared at him openly before making an almost-graceful recovery and fleeing to her bedroom, waving vaguely at the kitchen and muttering *need coffee* before she disappeared. Before her door closed, she followed up with a comment about *never wearing a dress again*, which I didn't think was for our ears and I sure as seas didn't understand.

Aster pulled on his human jeans – albeit reluctantly, the smug exhibitionist – and Cy slipped into the kitchen to make good on fulfilling Tessa's wish for whatever *coffee* was. Aster had seen it in Earth screencasts and was determined to try it, padding around the kitchen after Cy and wearing a satisfied, heavy-lidded smile.

I growled at him.

'Jealous, Mor?' he purred back at me. 'How unsurprising.'

'I'm not sure you have any kind of moral high ground right now, Aster,' Cy said mildly.

Aster gave his wide, taunting grin. 'No,' he said. 'But I have her taste on my tongue.'

My growl grew louder.

The starling sauntered out of the kitchen and towards me, where I was standing awkwardly near the couch. He pushed me down to sit with a palm to the chest, then traced a finger over my jaw. 'How badly do you want it?' he purred. 'How badly do you want to taste your *elyn*?'

I surged up and took his mouth, then gave a guttural groan as my mouth flooded with a tart sweetness that – if I was being entirely honest – I wanted to *bathe* in.

'She is the heavens,' Aster agreed hoarsely, slipping his tongue between my lips and letting my suckers flutter against it, tasting everything they could. I took his face in my hands and kissed him properly, letting him know that I wasn't just doing it to snatch a shadow of Tessa's taste, but that I'd missed him. He purred at me, his hands moving up and down my arms, soothing the anxiety I'd felt at our separation.

'Better?' he murmured against my lips.

'Not even slightly,' I said unevenly.

'So … You guys are together. Like, all three of you together. Or is Aster with both of you, but …?' Tessa trailed off.

We broke the kiss and looked up, almost guiltily. Tessa had dressed in loose grey sweatpants and a clinging black shirt, and it was somehow just as alluring as her bare skin. She studied us, her irises flashing a tempting green under the lights. Her expression was wary, but I could still scent her arousal. She shook her hair back over her shoulders; it was thick and curling, falling wild past her shoulders, spiralling into ringlets where it was damp with sweat.

I wanted to wrap it around my fingers.

Aster gave me a swift *don't be grouchy and fuck this up* look, and turned the full force of his most charming smile on Tessa. She blinked under the assault, taking a step back.

'I should introduce everyone properly,' Aster said smoothly, like the politician his parents always wanted him to be. 'And to answer your question, we *are* all together. All three of us. I know it isn't common on Earth, but we're not from here, and it works for us. Tessa, starlight, this is Morgan Eventide, Prince of Natare. And the beauty in the kitchen is Cy. He doesn't have another name because Mor and I named him, and we're not the most creative of beings.'

Tessa frowned in confusion. 'You named him?'

'I'm a cyborg,' Cy said matter-of-factly from the kitchen. 'Male Cyborg Number Four Million, Three Hundred and Seventy-Six Thousand, Nine Hundred and Fifty-Two, an organic and mechanic being activated on the sixth day of staryear thirteen billion, seventy-seven million –' Cy coughed as he caught himself. 'We are made, not born, and given numbers,' he finished in a rush. 'Morgan and Aster refused to call me by a number.'

Tessa's scent changed from slightly aroused to suddenly overwhelmed; she fiddled nervously with a thin silver chain around one wrist. 'You're a cyborg,' she repeated faintly.

Cy nodded, and slid open the simple control panel on his forearm, holding it up so Tessa could see. Lights flickered; one blinked in time with his heartbeat.

Tessa swallowed audibly, then made her way to the couch on shaky legs.

Cy made a quiet keening sound, his eyes fixed on Tessa. His scanners would pick up the physical signs of her distress; I couldn't see her heart race or her muscles tense, but I could scent her fear. It made every instinct in my body kick into overdrive; I wanted to wrap her in my arms and eliminate the source of it.

Except in this case, the source was *us*.

My chest gave a soft rumble.

Aster gave me a sharp look, then went to take Cy in his arms. 'It's all right, handsome,' he murmured. 'She just needs time.'

For a being that wasn't supposed to feel emotion, Cy was surprisingly good at them, but the more complex ones like Tessa must have been feeling – the mix of confusion and disbelief and wariness – were more difficult for him to understand and process. Aster and I had reassured him a thousand times that it wasn't because he was part machine – *all* beings found emotions difficult to recognise.

I was certainly having an interesting time with mine.

'Why don't you finish making the coffee?' Aster said, kissing Cy's cheek then stepping back to give him space. 'Tessa looks like she could use a hot drink, and I'm dying to try it.'

Cy shot him a look that said *I know exactly what you're doing* but did as Aster suggested, and soon the kitchen was filled with the scents of heating milk and ground roasted beans.

It smelled pretty good, actually.

Tessa studied me warily; I stared blatantly back. She deserved to be stared at. She was pretty, with a heart-shaped face and some light freckles dusting her nose. Her lips were luscious, small and perfectly shaped.

My hearts thumped against my ribs.

'If he's a cyborg, and Aster turns into ... *darkness*, apparently, then what are you?' she asked me bluntly.

'I think we should save me for another time,' I said.

'I'm a starling. His kind is called Enterocti – he's one of the many kinds of cephalopod,' Aster said helpfully, settling on the edge of the couch, far enough away from Tessa that he wouldn't crowd her.

Tessa blinked at me. 'He doesn't look like a fucking octopus.'

'He can change forms, like me,' Aster explained. 'His top half is always like that, including the scowl. But from the waist down, it's all tentacles.'

I rubbed my temples. 'Thanks, Aster.'

'We should be honest, shouldn't we?' he said, giving me his most infuriating grin. Usually when he gave me that smile I'd drag him into the pool and fuck him senseless. His grin widened, and his eyes hooded; he knew exactly what he was doing. He always did. 'Show Tessa your hands.'

'Aster –' I started.

'What's on his hands?' Tessa said, frowning.

It was possibly the most adorable expression I'd ever seen; every possessive and protective instinct I had rose to simmer beneath my skin. *By the seas*, I prayed silently. *Keep it together. Keep it together.*

My species were simple. We liked hunting, eating, and mating, and sometimes all three at the same time. But both Aster and Cy had warned me that human customs were very different and far more complicated, and that our human *elyn* would be unlikely to appreciate me dragging them into the nearest body of water and feeding them raw fish, no matter how much I might want to.

'He can't shift *everything*,' Aster said, answering Tessa. 'I can't, either. I can't change my eyes. Morgan keeps suckers in certain places; his palms, his fingers –' his eyes dropped to my mouth '– and his tongue.'

Tessa's frown deepened. She didn't look convinced, and her unease sharpened into something that began to push into fear.

I didn't want her to be afraid, especially not in her own home. I stood. 'Maybe we should just go,' I said quietly.

Cy dropped a spoon; it clattered noisily on the floor. 'But Morgan, she's our –'

'Do you want us to go, Tessa?' Aster said, his voice serious.

Tessa didn't answer. Her chin was tilted up, and her eyes were travelling over me. They lingered on my arms, my shoulders, then her gaze traced the lines of my face, so tangible I could almost feel it in a brush of silken fingertips.

A rumbling growl escaped me before I could stop it, and my whole body went tense as I struggled not to shift back to my trueform under my *elyn*'s steady green gaze.

'Morgan,' Aster said warningly.

I rumbled back at him.

Tessa turned her eyes to Cy. 'Do you growl, too?' she said.

'No,' Cy answered. 'That sound is used by cephalopods when they are communicating underwater. Morgan sometimes forgets he's on terra, and that we're not his kind.'

'And Aster?'

Cy tilted his head. 'Starlings are made of light, and they live in space; they communicate without sound. Aster's vocal chords sometimes don't know what to do when he shifts, so he makes a purring sound when he's happy.'

Tessa considered that information. 'What else should I know?'

I bit my lip, hiding a smile. Clever female.

Cy nodded. 'Morgan's grandmother is a seer. She told us we had a fourth – our *elyn* – and gave us a partial biostamp. I found three lifeforms – three in the entire *universe* – who the stamp could fit. We went to the other two first. They were ... They were not our *elyn*. So now we're here. For you.'

Her eyes went wide. 'Your *ee-lin*?' she repeated, tasting the word. 'What does that mean?'

'Many religions believe that every planet, every star, every moon and asteroid and swirl of space dust has its own place in the universe, its own divine orbit and its own foretold path. They think that when everything is in its place, the universe makes music.' Aster's voice was unexpectedly quiet, as if he were actually considering his words. I blinked in surprise; he wasn't religious. Perhaps finding Tessa had made him reconsider. 'The believers extend this concept to personal universes – the place and time that you inhabit, the beings you interact with, even one's own bodily form.' His eyes glowed. 'Earth has its own version of the concept – *musica mundana*, the music of the spheres, and *musica humana*, the music that unifies the body and soul. You even have soulmates, your version of *elyn* – a being fated to bring harmony to a personal universe; the last part fitting into a whole, the balancing note of a perfect song.' His gaze flickered to me, then Cy, then went back to Tessa. 'The believers are fairly vague on exactly *how* an *elyn* brings harmony, saying that it's different for every personal universe and different for every *elyn*. It certainly seems to vary between species. But one thing they all agree on is that an *elyn* is precious. Treasured. Revered.'

Tessa shook her head. 'I haven't been to church since I was ten, I can't sing to save myself, and I'm none of those things,' she declared. 'I don't fit in my own world, let alone anyone else's.' She paused. 'What are you expecting, exactly?'

'There's no expectation,' I said roughly. I would die before I'd take an unwilling mate. 'We just had to meet you. To see you. To spend some time with you, and to convince you to come with us if we can. But there's no expectation.'

'You want me to come *with* you?' she said, incredulous. 'As in, away from here? Away from my apartment? Away from the *city*?'

'Yes.' I stared back at her, unwavering. 'As in, away from *Earth*.'

She made a helpless gesture with her hands. 'I just met you! You might be murderers, traffickers, anything at all!' She twisted her lips. 'You're trying to tell me that you're not human, not like me, but that I'll bring some kind of harmony to your world? You don't *know* me. I don't know *you*. All I wanted was *one bloody dance*!'

'Aster has known you quite intimately, apparently.'

She flushed a beautiful pink, her nostrils flaring. 'Fuck you,' she said, glaring at me. 'That doesn't *mean* anything.'

'Ouch,' Aster muttered.

I snorted. 'If you were my species, you'd already be bonded.'

She set her jaw. 'I'm *not* your species! I'm human. And we don't believe that a quick fuck on the couch equals *destiny*.'

Aster's eyes narrowed. '*Quick?*'

I laughed out loud at his expression. 'Were you in a rush, starling?'

He crossed his arms. 'If it was too *quick* for you, Tessa, I'm ready and willing to try again.'

The scent of sea lilies washed over me. I took a deep breath, biting my bottom lip hard enough to draw blue blood. 'She likes that idea.'

Tessa's eyes flickered to me. 'What?' she said, startled.

'I can smell you,' I rumbled. 'Your scent is like a sea lily. I've never known a female to smell like you.'

'So I have good taste in perfume,' she snapped.

'Oh, no, starlight,' Aster purred. 'That's not all he can scent.'

Tessa stared at me.

'When males of my species bond, scent is all they know,' I said. 'Scent tells us everything – whether the female is sweet or fierce or vicious, whether she's strong enough to raise younglings. It tells us whether she's likely to kill us during the coupling, or whether we'll survive to hunt another season.' I took a deep breath, raking her in. 'Sea lilies are resilient. They survive through storms, their stems sinking beneath the sand and acting as an anchor deep beneath the waves. Their scent is heady and seductive; they are the preferred flower of the sea bees. And they are the symbol of our most important goddess.' I didn't tell her it was the symbol of our *fertility* goddess. 'They are my favourite flower.'

She gripped the couch cushions, swallowing, but she didn't drop her gaze. The blush on her cheeks spread down her neck, but I kept my eyes on hers.

'We know you are human, *elyn*, but we are all something different, and we all have different ways. You might not know me, but I already have everything I need to know. I found it the moment I walked through that door.'

I turned away deliberately, fearing that if I didn't, I'd drown in her gaze.

There was a moment of silence as I sank down – uninvited – into a cream armchair. I was too wide for it – my shoulders pressed uncomfortably against its wings – but I had to do *something* to stop myself shifting forms.

'Well then,' Aster said brightly. 'Now you know how bossy Morgan is, so that's pretty much everything.'

Cy frowned, pouring hot milk into mugs. 'Aster, I don't think that's true.'

'Show me your hands,' Tessa said, and got up off the couch.

I narrowed my eyes. 'What?'

She gestured impatiently. 'Aster said you had suckers on your hands. Show me.'

I clenched my fingers into fists.

'Mor,' Aster said softly. 'Show her.'

I ground my jaw.

'It won't be like last time,' Aster coaxed. 'Tessa wasn't scared of me, was she?'

'Tessa was very much scared of you,' Tessa retorted. 'What do you mean by *last time*?'

Cy carried four mugs to Tessa's small table and placed them down with a quiet *thump*. 'Like we said, I found three beings who matched the partial biostamps Morgan's grandmother gave us. We went to the other two before we came here. The first ...' Cy glanced at Aster and me. 'The first could not understand that we could have loved each other *and* him. He wanted ... He only wanted me.' Cy blushed, his cheeks a delicious dark red, giving Tessa a prime example of *why* the male had fixated on the cyborg. 'I could never leave Aster and Morgan, and I didn't feel anything for him anyway, so ... Well, we left. The second ...' Cy's eyes flickered to me, his brow furrowed in concern.

The owner of the second biostamp had liked me best. She was Nautilina, a cephalopod being like me, though a different kind. She was beautiful, confident, and warm, and her attention had stoked my ego – until I realised that it wasn't *me* she wanted, but rather the title of Princess Consort. I was so fooled by her flattery that I'd been convinced I could win her around into a genuine partnership; that notion had swiftly shattered when she'd shuddered in fear – and hatred – at the sight of my shifted humanoid legs and demanded that I stay permanently in my trueform.

It didn't work that way on my planet, Natare; we might have been born with tentacles, but we shifted whenever we felt like it, and the only preference placed on form was personal. Some Enterocti spent most of their lives in their humanoid form, because it was most comfortable for them; some lived permanently in aqua, and no one minded either way.

She had shaken my belief, both in the universe and in myself; I'd allowed myself to be blinded by pride. Nothing had happened between us, not even a kiss, but I was shocked by how close I'd come to drawing my mates into a poisonous bond with a female who despised humanoids.

The irony was that I might now have the opposite problem: that the gorgeous female before me might recoil from my non-humanoid trueform.

'It did not go well,' I said shortly.

Tessa studied my face. 'And you think this won't *go well*, either.'

I tipped my head back. 'I'm imagining not.'

She pursed her lips. 'Why don't we find out?' She held out her hand.

She had small hands, with slender, tapered fingers. They were elegantly shaped, but two of them were marred by small burns. I glowered at them. Those burns didn't belong on my *elyn's* fingers. I hated the idea that she could be hurt.

Tessa waited.

I extended my hand and opened my fingers.

She exhaled. 'Fuck me sideways,' she muttered to no one in particular, tipping her chin up to stare at the ceiling for a moment. 'If I'm having a breakdown, this sure isn't the hallucination I would have expected. I always preferred fantasy to sci-fi.'

Suckers grew in a cluster on my palm, then in a line up each finger. Tessa dipped her chin back down and stared at them.

'Oh, Mor,' Aster said sadly.

The suckers were currently a bright, fearful red.

It was something I couldn't hide, not in the way I could control my expressions. The suckers gave away exactly what I was feeling, at every moment of the day or night.

'Do they change colour?' Tessa said, noticing the shade flicker.

'With his emotions,' Cy said.

Tessa's eyebrows rose. 'Like a mood ring,' she murmured. 'A whole-body mood ring. Some of our cephalopods do the same thing.' She reached out, then froze. 'Can I touch them?'

'I –' I stopped. 'Sorry, *what*?'

'Can I touch them?' she repeated.

I stared at her. 'You *want* to touch them?'

'I can touch the ones on your tongue if you'd prefer,' she said tartly.

My cock twitched. A growl escaped before I could stop it.

'Okay, so not the ones in your mouth, got it,' she said.

'That's his *happy* growl,' Aster said.

'How can you tell?' she muttered.

He gestured at my hands.

The suckers were varying from moment to moment, from their fearful red to a deeper maroon made of desire. They fluctuated more swiftly the closer that Tessa moved towards me; when she was so close I could touch her, they fixed on dark scarlet. She touched the tip of her finger to the tip of mine; I shuddered with want, holding my hand open with difficulty. She traced the sucker on the pad of my finger, so delicately that I could barely feel it.

My cock went rock hard, trapped painfully behind the confines of the odd human clothing.

She circled the rim, then brushed her fingertip over its cup. I sank my teeth into my bottom lip. I could taste her through the sucker, taste the salt of her sweat and, fainter, Aster's. I growled as I imagined her encased in my arms, imagining tasting *every* part of her. I'd need her to myself the first time, but after that, I could work with my mates to please her.

To *worship* her.

'Your teeth are sharp,' she observed, withdrawing her hand.

I pulled them out of my lip, tasting blood. 'My kind ... Enterocti are not gentle. We are hunters, made to chase sharks and spearfish and huge ocean crocodiles.'

'And they *bite*,' Aster added, with a heavy-eyed smile.

Tessa frowned.

I shot Aster a glare. 'We bite to seal our mating bonds. Enterocti females try to attract every male they can when they are ready for breeding, and the venom from the male bite means the female will focus on him alone, rather than taking multiple partners, which usually ends in battle and a whole lot of blood.'

'How does that work with you and Cy?' she said, her eyes going to Aster.

He shrugged. 'We're not entirely sure. We were about to complete the bonding ceremony when Morgan's grandmother had her vision. We decided to wait until ...' He trailed off.

'Until you found your *elyn*,' Tessa finished. She turned her frown to me. 'Does that mean you'd want to bite me, too?'

I gave a sharp nod. I wanted it so badly I could almost feel her skin give way beneath my fangs.

She eyed me thoughtfully. 'Do you have eight ... legs?'

'*Arms*,' I said. 'Or limbs. And yes, eight.'

'One doubles as a mating shaft,' Aster added helpfully.

I rubbed my temples. 'Aster,' I growled. 'One thing at a time.'

Aster winked at an astonished Tessa. 'Why wait?' he purred. 'It's one of the best parts.'

'THE COFFEE IS GETTING cold,' I said. It was partly to distract Tessa, who was starting to look overwhelmed again, and partly because it was true. Though there were some outliers, the Earth's internet suggested that the ideal temperature for serving coffee was between seventy and eighty degrees Celsius, and the liquid in the mugs had dropped to sixty-eight point five.

I'd found Tessa's sugar pot, and I cautiously added a spoonful of the tiny, sparkling grains to my cup. The internet had also suggested that sweet coffee was better for newcomers to the drink, which didn't exactly inspire confidence.

Though it did smell good.

I lifted the cup to my lips as Tessa sat at the table, wrapping her hands around her mug. Aster sat next to her, and Morgan opposite; he eyed his cup warily. Morgan was the bravest person I knew, but he wasn't the most adventurous eater.

I took a cautious sip.

And put my mug back down.

Tessa pressed her lips together, hiding a smile. 'Is this the first time you've had coffee?'

I nodded, trying to analyse the emotion sitting between my chest and stomach. *Shyness*, I decided. I'd felt it before, when I'd first met Morgan. I loved him, but he was overwhelming, standing taller than most beings, with wide shoulders and a fierce scowl.

And the *muscles*. I glanced at him, taking in the human t-shirt stretched taut over his biceps and chest, the lovely, hard planes sculpted over countless hours of swimming and hunting.

Mmm.

He raised an eyebrow at me, his expression amused.

I took another hasty sip of my coffee.

It got better on the third sip, when my tongue could move past the bitterness and begin to taste the flavours. Nutty, I decided. Nutty and smoky, underlain by the sweetness of the sugar.

Morgan took one mouthful, wrinkled his nose, and pushed his mug towards Aster.

Tessa laughed under her breath.

Aster beamed. 'This is everything I hoped it would be,' he said, smiling at his two cups. I scanned his form out of habit. Because Aster's organic body was entirely made, the parameters had a habit of changing. I was trained as an engineer, not a doctor, but I'd worked out some rough standards over time. His temperature was normal, rising and falling between forty and forty-two degrees Celsius, and his heart rate was also fluctuating, as usual. Morgan's hearts were racing, but he was looking at Tessa, so I put it down to fear or desire; his core temperature was normal at thirty-four degrees.

Tessa was a perfect human thirty-seven degrees. Her heart rate was slightly high, but she was clearly still nervous, her fingers trembling slightly on the table. I picked up my mug and ran some quick internal scans. I could see that she'd broken a toe some years ago; it had healed unevenly, so it was possible she'd not known it was broken. She had scar tissue in several places on her abdomen, and I could see the lines on her belly where she'd been carefully cut open: endometriosis, which was regrowing. A healing wand could fix it, but I'd need to take her to the ship; I hadn't thought to bring one with me. I frowned as my scanners looked deeper. She had a contraceptive device implanted in her uterus; it needed to be replaced. She'd have to be careful if she didn't want infection or to risk a pregnancy.

I forced my eyes to my cup; I didn't want her to think I was staring, and I knew that seeing inside another being was the kind of intrusion that was not always appreciated outside a medical context. Morgan and Aster were used to it; I sometimes got lost in them, fascinated by their skin or the shine of their hair or the way that muscle joined and moved. Tessa was softer, rounder, but no less compelling. I liked how smooth her skin looked, and the freckles on her nose and her arms. I liked the ringlets in the underside of her hair and the shape of her fingernails. I liked the heaviness of her breasts and the way her waist tapered in a deep curve.

Aster cleared his throat, drawing me back to the table. 'Tell us about your life, Tessa.'

She blinked. 'There's not much to tell.'

'Liar,' Aster said comfortably. 'Even the littlest of lives are full of stories. You studied Art History, and you want to study more. You manage a busy shop. Did you grow up in this city?'

Tessa shook her head. 'I grew up just outside another city in the south,' she said. 'My cousin Rian still lives there. I came here when I was nineteen.'

'What made you move?' Aster said.

Tessa looked at her cup. 'My parents and my younger brother were caught in a house fire. They died.'

She blinked rapidly. Her heart thumped unevenly and her knuckles went white on her cup. I reached out to touch her – to comfort her – but stopped myself, pulling my hand back and dropping it into my lap.

'It's ok,' she said to me, her voice soft. 'It was a long time ago now. Eight years.'

'But you still grieve,' Morgan rumbled.

She gave a one-shouldered shrug. 'How could I not?'

'What were their names?' Aster said.

'Estelle and Stephen,' Tessa answered. 'And my brother was Thomas.'

'So you moved away from home,' Morgan prompted, after a moment's silence. Neither Morgan nor Aster offered condolences. For a moment, I struggled with why – it was polite, wasn't it, to offer your sorrow? When I thought about it further, I supposed they were right – how could words help in the face of such an immeasurable loss? What if it wasn't something Tessa wanted to dwell on, or discuss with strangers?

I wondered if I'd ever get to the point where I knew what I should feel, and what to say.

A soft vibration from my control panel distracted me from that thought. I ran my fingers over it, not needing to check the count down on the alarm I'd set. I knew how much longer we had left, right down to the Earth nanosecond.

Six hours.

My eyes flickered to Morgan and Aster; Morgan gave an almost-imperceptible grimace in response, and Aster lifted his chin, determination flashing in his golden eyes. I swallowed, then turned my attention back to Tessa.

'I'd gotten offers from a few universities. I chose one that was far away from my hometown and my school friends. My friends didn't know what to do after the fire – they were too young to know what to say when someone had lost everything – and I was resentful that they couldn't offer what I needed. Even though I was also too young to know what that was.' She gave another half-shrug as my heart constricted. 'I know now that it wasn't their fault, but at the time … At the time, all I could think was that they weren't there for me in the way that I wanted. In the way that I needed. So I withdrew, and when I moved, it completed the cut.' She took another sip of her coffee, her hand trembling slightly.

I analysed the emotions flowing through me. Sadness and compassion were easy enough to identify. Empathy was more difficult, but strongly felt – I could sympathise with such a big change, after all. Something newer – something surprising – was my wish to make it better, to take her in my arms and stroke her hair. Not to make her forget, but to let her know that I was there. That I'd support her. Hold her if she wanted to cry.

Tessa didn't look like she cried very often.

'And you completed your degree?' Aster said.

She nodded. 'And my Honours year.'

Aster dipped his chin in acknowledgement; I had to do a quick internet trawl to understand what that meant. Morgan had done military training at an academy on Natare, and my kind were trained and streamlined into specialist areas from birth, but Aster had collected a list of formal educational accomplishments as long as my arm from across the universe. He'd had two thousand years to do it, to be fair. He often said that time passed slowly before he met us.

I wondered how quickly time would pass now, knowing Tessa was in our universe. Morgan and I wouldn't be allowed back to Earth for five years – that was the law for visiting planets that hadn't signed the intergalactic constitution – but no one could stop Aster returning if Tessa didn't come with us. He was made of starlight, after all, and could travel just as fast through space, no ship needed. There was almost nothing that could keep him out of a place he wanted to be.

'And your job? What's it like?'

Tessa looked startled. 'It's ... fine, I suppose. I like some of it, I love some of it, and I hate a lot of it. But the money is ok –' she winced, possibly belying those words '– and it's close by. I like living here. It's close to the city centre, and there are some nice parks ...' She trailed off as she tried to find something else.

'Do you live with a friend?' Morgan growled. 'Or a mate?'

Tessa narrowed her eyes at him. 'Humans don't have *mates*. Not outside romance novels, at least. And yes, Maeve is my friend. Aster would have seen her at Advena. She manages the bar there. Do I get to ask the questions now?'

She lifted her chin, as if waiting for a refusal, then looked surprised when Aster settled back in his chair and sipped his coffee. 'Of course. We'll answer anything you want to know.'

'If you're not from Earth, then how are you speaking English?' she challenged.

Aster's lips curled. 'You're trying to poke holes in our story,' he said, his tone approving. 'Unfortunately, that's an easy one.'

Tessa's gaze turned to me.

I wasn't sure why. But I liked her soft green eyes falling on me, and she'd asked me questions before, so I answered this one, too.

'Aster,' I said quietly. 'The scent of starlings can alter neural pathways in organic beings. One way Aster can use this is by making himself a kind of universal translator. Anything he understands, you understand.'

She blinked. 'So if Aster left, I wouldn't be able to understand you anymore?'

Aster shook his head. 'My presence has already changed your brain. You'd understand Morgan even if I wasn't here now. Of course, Cy is leaving part of it out,' he said, arching a straight black brow at me. 'He wanted to do things the old-fashioned way.'

'The old-fashioned way?' Tessa asked.

I looked at my cup. 'I learned some Earth languages on the way here.'

Aster snorted. 'He's being modest. He learned Mandarin, Hindi, Spanish, French, Arabic, and Russian, along with English. You don't need any kind of translator with Cy.'

Tessa's eyes widened. 'You learned seven languages,' she said flatly.

I bit my lip. 'Also Bengali and a few others, just in case.'

She slumped back in her chair. 'Why? Why do that, if Aster could just change my brain?'

I shrugged as I tried to analyse my feelings. Discomfort, shyness again, panic that I might have done the wrong thing. 'I thought it would be one way I could try to know you. Languages can teach a lot about culture and ways of life. Language is the way that beings think. I thought it might help me understand you. I thought it might be … nice,' I finished lamely.

'It *is* nice,' she said. 'It's ... It's the nicest thing anyone has done for me in a very long time.' She looked away.

Oh, that was *definitely* sadness welling up my throat. Sadness that no one had done more for her than learn a few words. Indignance, that no one had tried. She was our *elyn*. She was perfect. The other humans should have been falling over themselves to love her. I waited, considering emotions as they churned in my chest and stomach. Anger reared its head. Not at Tessa, but at her species. Why was she living here with a friend and not a mate? Who wouldn't want to be with her?

Aster touched my hand, bringing me back. 'What's your next question?'

'How did you get here?'

'Our ship,' Morgan answered.

'*Morgan's* ship,' Aster corrected.

Tessa sipped her coffee. 'What's it like?'

'Small,' Morgan said.

Aster snorted. 'It's four times larger than the crafts generally used for private cross-sector travel. Morgan has odd notions about size.'

'How not-small is it?'

'It has the cockpit, a kitchen, a bathroom, the pool, a rec room, a transporter, a few storerooms, and our bedroom.' I paused. 'We sleep together – well, Morgan and I do; Aster has a tendency to float ...' I trailed off.

'Sounds cosy,' Tessa said lightly. 'You said you've been travelling for five straight years? What did you do all that time?'

'Morgan and Cy drive the show,' Aster said. 'Morgan pilots; Cy maintains the systems. When he's not flying, Morgan lazes in the pool and rouses himself to fuck anyone careless enough to dip a toe in the water stupid.'

Morgan gave a rumbling growl – an amused one – and Tessa almost spat her coffee out. 'And you?'

'I read and watch screencasts and generally lounge around looking beautiful.'

She wrinkled her nose at him playfully. 'Useful.'

'Come now, Tessa,' Aster said, mock-serious. 'You of all people should know the value of beauty for beauty's sake.'

'I'm sure that's what Cy and Morgan think as they do all the work.'

'Cruel *elyn*,' he purred. 'I give them things, too. Blow jobs. Cups of tea.'

Tessa blushed a beautiful deep pink. 'How long ... How long have you been together? How did you meet?'

Morgan glanced at Aster. 'Around eleven of your Earth years, I think.'

Aster gave a soft smile, and leaned across to capture Morgan's mouth with his. My heart pounded at the sight; it always did. 'My parents didn't know what to do with me, so they sent me to Natare as an envoy.'

'That lasted all of a day,' Morgan said wryly.

'I'm still an advisor,' Aster said with a mock-pout. 'Just unofficially. Apparently, a diplomatic envoy fucking a member of the royal family they're supposed to be working with is considered a conflict of interest.'

'Who would have thought,' Tessa said dryly. 'And Cy?'

Aster smiled at me across the table; his foot traced up my calf under the table. 'Morgan had to visit Machina, Cy's home, as part of a diplomatic corps,' he began. I flushed slightly; they loved telling this story.

'Aster got bored and went for a walk,' Morgan went on fondly. 'There are no bars on Machina, no drug dens, no underbelly

... I thought he couldn't possibly get into trouble. But Aster is Aster.'

'I snuck into one of their training facilities – like your universities.' Aster took the story back up. 'Cyborgs are programmed to a certain extent, but their systems adapt to knowledge. Their facilities divide students into disciplinary areas until they become experts. They use a mix of instruction by teachers, automated learning, and downloads straight into their systems to maintain the balance between organic learning and system-prompted fact retention. I was wandering past a class on intergalactic systems when I noticed a particularly gorgeous red head. But unlike the rest of the students – and the teacher – he wasn't focused on his work. He was plugged in, but he was noticing me right back.'

My memory was always almost-perfect – allowing for the effects of emotion – but that memory was clearer than most. Aster had looked slightly different then – he'd been less practised at controlling his light, so it had spilled from beneath his skin in a soft glow – and I remembered seeing him walk past the doorway. Remembered the jolt of feeling that had sparked up my spine. Remembered my blood rushing, my heart pounding, my chest constricting. Remembered the *need* to get up from my cubicle and follow him, to meet him, remembered the way the unfamiliar emotions had swept through me like a storm, and how overwhelming the world suddenly became, knowing that someone who could make me feel all those things existed within it.

'All cyborgs are made beautiful, but I think you'll agree, Tessa, that Cy is *particularly* beautiful,' Aster went on. I flushed again, though I'd heard the praise countless times. 'But it wasn't just that. Cyborgs regulate their children's emotional development to ensure that complex feelings like attraction – and love – never take hold. But here was this beautiful being, and ... *Well.*'

'Aster was the loveliest thing I'd ever seen,' I said matter-of-factly. 'I didn't know what I was feeling. I didn't know what to *do*. But I knew that I wanted to look at him more –'

'And Aster loves being looked at,' Morgan interjected dryly.

'– so I left the class and followed him. He walked to the edge of campus, then stopped. He asked me what I wanted.'

'He said *I don't know what to call it*,' Aster said softly. 'So I said –'

'*Can you show me without words?*' I shook my head. 'Of all the lines in the universe.'

'It worked,' Aster said, smiling smugly. 'A moment later, the stars were singing and I was being thoroughly kissed. I was quite happy about it.'

Tessa looked as if she was trying to hold back a smile. 'Morgan wasn't jealous?'

Aster snorted. 'Morgan fell in love with Cy the moment he saw him.'

'And you, Cy?' she said softly.

'My biological response to Morgan was as strong as my response to Aster,' I said. 'It felt ... right.'

'And how long ago was that?'

'Seven Earth years.'

'If you've all been together that long, why are you here now?' Tessa said slowly. 'You're clearly happy. It doesn't seem like you need anything more.'

'We are happy,' Aster said carefully. 'What we have is incredible, and we are all aware of how lucky we are.'

'But an *elyn* isn't something you ignore, Tessa,' Morgan said. 'An *elyn* is something to fight for.' He shook his head slightly.

'Knowing that you exist – knowing that you're as perfect for us as we are for you? Knowing that the universe made us this way?' He shrugged. 'How could we ever forget that? How could we ever not *try*?'

'Even cyborgs believe in balance,' I offered shyly. 'It's as close as we get to the divine.'

Tessa toyed with the handle of her mug. 'I've never balanced anything.'

Morgan tilted his head and studied her face. 'Maybe you just haven't found the right weights,' he said.

'There was one more thing,' Aster said. 'Along with the bio-stamp, Morgan's grandmother gave us something in code. She said our *elyn* would need to hear it.'

Tess frowned. 'What is it?'

Aster picked up his mug. 'Do you know what *fifteen point ninety K* means, Tessa?'

TESSA

Fifteen point ninety K.

I tried to control my expression, but I could tell that they knew it meant something to me. I curled my fingers around my mug and drained my coffee.

15.90K.

My fucking ring size.

I knew, because my ex had asked me to find out. He'd held the possibility of *rings* over my head like a perpetual carrot. Like if I could be *better*, *thinner*, *nicer* to his disgusting friends, more *polite* to his leering father and disapproving mother, then just *maybe* I'd be lucky enough that he'd *deign* to slide an engagement band over my fourth finger.

He hadn't, obviously. But I'd stayed with him so much longer than I should have because of the chance of that shiny fucking carat. As if having a rock on my finger would somehow fix me, and suddenly make me *belong*. As if having it would suddenly make me *happy*, fix our problems. As if a *ring* would mean happily ever after.

I liked to think that I'd been pretty calm so far. That watching Aster *dissolve into black light and float on the ceiling* was enough to send anyone straight to the hospital, and I hadn't whimpered and burst into tears. That seeing Cy *open his arm to reveal a control panel* was the kind of shit you scoffed at in b-grade movies, and I hadn't fallen over. That touching the *sucker on Morgan's palms and finding it warm and moving* was one of the most surreal moments of my life, but instead of fainting on the couch, I'd wanted to touch it *more* and had been oddly invested in the thought of feeling it flutter against my skin.

I liked to think that I'd been doing pretty damn well, thank you very much. Every single thing that had happened to me in the last few hours was utterly insane, and I was still standing. Metaphorically, at least.

I couldn't let *this* be the thing that broke me.

'You know,' Aster said, watching me closely.

I could feel three pairs of eyes on me. 'I don't want to talk about it,' I said shortly.

'Then we will not,' Morgan said decisively, and I almost fell in love with him on the spot. One of the first things Maeve had drilled into me after I'd moved in with her was that I didn't owe anyone an explanation for *anything*, let alone my trauma, and that my boundaries weren't rude – they were necessary. 'Do you have other questions, Tessa?'

Only a million or so. 'Let's play a game,' I said brightly, pushing back my chair. A game would divide their attention, give me breathing space. 'I'll find something.'

I still wasn't exactly sure why I hadn't kicked them out. If I was honest, it had a lot to do with Aster's panty-melting grin and Morgan's unreal muscles and Cy's impossible beauty, but they'd also piqued my curiosity in the best possible way. I mean – *they literally were not human*. Who wouldn't be intrigued? Who wouldn't want to spend time with them? It didn't mean I was considering doing anything else. That would be mad.

Wouldn't it?

I also simply liked them, I supposed. More than I'd liked anyone new in a long time. If I was *completely* honest, I wouldn't mind hearing Morgan growl again, either. The last one had made me throb in a way that was almost embarrassing. I didn't think I could come from *sound*, but I was willing to give it a try.

I wondered if he growled like that in bed. If he'd growl as he thrust, growl as he kissed, growl as his mouth moved over my skin. I flushed thinking about it; heat flared in other places, too. Would he fucked with his cock, or with — what had Aster called it? — his *mating shaft*?

I shivered.

'Uh, Tessa, starlight,' Aster said carefully. 'Remember that whatever you're thinking about right now, Morgan can *smell* it.'

I looked back up to see Morgan's unwavering blue stare fixed on my face, his nostrils flared. He seemed suddenly taller, his shoulders suddenly broader; he filled the room.

I blushed properly, mortified, finally realising what they'd meant. 'He can *smell* it?'

'Mmm,' Aster said, studying his mug as if it were the most interesting thing in the world. 'His senses are ridiculous. The moment you're hurt, or, um, *not*, he'll know about it.'

'You can smell ...' I trailed off, trying to think of another time I'd been so embarrassed and coming up short.

'Your slick,' Morgan grated out bluntly.

'Oh, fucking *hell*,' I said, sure that my face had never been so hot.

'Like I said. Sea lilies blooming,' he growled.

That didn't help matters; my body thrilled at the sound and my core turned molten. 'A game,' I squeaked, and all but ran to my bedroom to escape.

I lurked in the darkness of my room for a good ten minutes, trying to calm myself down. It didn't really work; all I wanted to do was slide my hand between my legs to take the edge off. Instead, I rummaged around in my cupboard and found a board game.

'If I still like them after playing this, it'll be a miracle,' I muttered.

I took a deep breath and squared my shoulders before I marched back out to the living room.

Oh, fuck, I thought desperately. *I am so fucked.*

Morgan had found my tablet and clearly my passcode – the thought didn't worry me the way that it should have – and was flicking through a social media app, his huge form stretched out along the couch like he belonged there. Aster was washing up while Cy was perusing the kitchen cupboards.

'Tessa, Aster wants to try cupcakes,' he called. 'We'll replace everything afterwards, but can I use –'

'Use whatever you want,' I blurted. 'All the cooking stuff is mine. Maeve exists solely on takeaway and men's tears.'

Cy turned and gave me a smile that made my knees weak. 'I know,' he said. 'I can see your fingerprints on the boxes. Hers are only on the kettle, the fridge, and the coffee machine. What flavour cupcakes?'

'What's your favourite, Tessa?' Aster said, flicking the tea towel over his shoulder.

'Um,' I answered, my brain struggling to complete its most basic functions while watching the pair of them in the kitchen, moving around each other with the easy grace born of long familiarity. It was comfortable and natural and possibly the most beautiful and surreal thing I'd ever seen. 'Chocolate.'

Cy pulled a packet of cocoa from the cupboard. 'Chocolate it is.'

'Your species has had *two* world wars?' Morgan rumbled. He looked up from the tablet and glared, as if it was my fault. 'Did you not learn from the first one?'

'You've found the internet, I see,' I said, perching on the arm of the chair. I shook the Monopoly box at him. 'This is more fun than a comments section.'

His eyes narrowed. It was easy to see him as a hunter when he looked like that; if there was a predator in the room, it was Morgan. He flowed off the couch in one easy motion; I swallowed when I found him closer, bringing the scent of salt and sunlight. My body liked it just as much as Aster's spice and woodsmoke, and I tried to ignore my ovaries, which were screaming something along the lines of *must breed immediately*.

'Tessa,' he growled.

'I know, I know,' I muttered. 'Could you pretend to not notice?'

He bared his teeth. 'Why would I do *that*?'

'So I don't die of mortification.'

He leaned closer; I froze. 'You could let me take care of you instead.'

I tried very hard not to imagine what that would be like while I convinced my heart to stop racing.

Before I could say something stupid – well, *stupider* – Aster came to my rescue. 'How do you play?'

I stared at him.

'The *game*, Tessa,' he grinned. 'What are the rules?'

I looked blankly at the box in my hand, my mind suddenly empty of everything that had happened before tonight, taking the rules of Monopoly with it.

'I've just found them,' Cy said, his eyes closed, two eggs in one hand and a wooden spoon in the other. It didn't help me think; Cy with his eyes closed was impossibly lovely. His skin had a pale glow to it, as if he's been lifted straight from a Pre-Raphaelite painting, though no artist could possibly capture the perfection of his features, the divinity of his slight blush. He frowned, a line appearing between his fair brows; I assumed he was scanning the internet again somehow. 'Are you sure you want to play this game, Tessa? There seems to be a wealth of evidence suggesting it is the cause of many unnecessary family confrontations.'

'Are you scared of losing, Cy?' I said sweetly.

Aster chuckled. 'If you're picking on Cy because you think he's an easy mark, starlight, you should change your strategy. He's a professional.'

'A professional?' I pulled the coffee table away from the couches and folded down to the floor.

Cy shot Aster what might have been a dirty look, his lips slightly pursed. 'Aster is being facetious, as usual.'

'And you're being too modest, as always,' Aster retorted. He grinned at me, then moved to sit within arm's reach. I could feel the warmth of him immediately, like I was sitting near a heater. 'When Cy was kicked off Machina, he hacked their banking systems. He stole enough credits to last three lifetimes, then completely scrambled their code. They had to rewrite their systems entirely.' His voice rang with pride.

I sat up straight. 'You were kicked off your planet?'

Cy looked away, breaking the eggs into a bowl. 'I was given a chance to atone for my transgressions. I declined, and was exiled.'

'Atone for *what* transgressions?'

When Cy didn't speak, Morgan answered for him. 'For us,' the blonde said roughly. 'For what we had, even in the very beginning. For what he felt. Machina's current government leans towards their mechanic – rather than their organic – side. They align more with programming and parts than with the blood in their veins and their ability to learn and change.'

'They wanted Cy to atone for the *flesh crimes* committed with us by having his programming reset.' Aster's voice went icy cold, though the air around him burned hotter, almost uncomfortably so. 'If he agreed, he wouldn't forget us, but any feeling he'd ever experienced would have been wiped.'

'I didn't want that,' Cy said to the mixing bowl. He looked across at us as Morgan sat next to Aster, opposite the board from me. 'I still don't know if what I feel is the same as what full organic beings feel. But I knew that I didn't want to lose my feelings, either way. And I'd be permanently shut down before I let them hurt Morgan and Aster.'

'So we abducted him,' Aster said with a wicked smile, his eyes lidded. 'Just like humans think aliens do here. But not before he crashed Machina's economy. The planet is *still* recovering.'

'Serves them right,' Morgan growled.

I ignored the throb between my legs that sound produced, though Morgan and Aster didn't. The former fixed me with a stare that would have melted my underwear if I'd had the courage to properly meet it, and Aster openly laughed, though in a husky way that thrilled up my spine as he shifted slightly closer to me. I ignored them, aiming for a dignity I absolutely did not feel as I set up the board. Cy put the cupcake batter in the oven and set the timer, then joined us on the floor, taking his place between me and Morgan.

I hadn't been close enough to catch his scent before. It washed over me now, all fresh linen and some kind of musky, masculine soap that had my heart pounding like it was trying to escape the cage of my ribs.

Cy recited the rules as if he knew them by heart. Aster and Morgan listened, apparently needing no clarification, though I supposed that if Morgan actually *was* a prince, and Aster *had* been his advisor, it was exactly the kind of thing they'd absorb without too much difficulty.

I pursed my lips. Perhaps I'd chosen the wrong game.

'Who goes first?' Aster said, stretching out in a way that had his dark curls almost spilling over my knee. I resisted the urge to run my fingers through his hair.

But only barely.

'Tessa does,' Cy said immediately.

I looked up to see Morgan's eyes hood and fix on mine. 'Tessa does,' he agreed, but I didn't think he was talking about going first in the game.

I closed my eyes for a moment. *You can't seriously be thinking about this,* my rational brain protested. *This is utter madness.*

Cy brushed my knee as he reached for the board, and my hormones went haywire.

Fucked, I thought. *I am so fucked.*

✧✧✧ ASTER

'HUMANS DON'T ACTUALLY DO this for fun,' I said. 'I think you're lying to us, Tessa.'

'I'm not lying,' she insisted, laughing. 'Humans spend hours doing this. The fun depends on who you do it with.'

'It is perfectly enjoyable,' Cy said solemnly.

'Because you're winning,' Morgan muttered.

'He's kicking your ass,' Tessa agreed smugly.

I didn't mention that the margin might have been closer if Morgan had been less distracted by the human sitting across the board from him. He was tracking her every movement, storing the slightest shift of weight or slide of her fingertip in his hunter's brain, building up a picture of his prey so that he might build the perfect trap.

I was still *almost* certain that he wouldn't eat her, though the look in his eyes suggested it could go either way.

She did smell deliciously edible. *Sea lilies blooming,* Morgan had said, and I agreed; though my senses weren't as sharp as his, her scent was floral. Her taste had faded on my tongue and I wanted my face back between her legs before it went completely. I'd managed to manoeuvre closer to her during the game so that my head was against her side, my arm curled all the way behind her, my hand stroking the outside of her thigh. It wasn't comfortable – not even the tiniest bit – but I gave exactly zero fucks as she tentatively rested her arm on my shoulder and Morgan shot me a look that said if he didn't get Tessa tonight, he was definitely going to have *me*.

I was almost certain that he wouldn't eat *me*, either.

I'd given up on the game long ago, and was cheating to keep Tessa's bank full, and occasionally shifting the air temperature so the dice landed one way rather than the other. Both Morgan and Cy knew exactly what I was doing – I always cheated, no matter what we played – but neither of them said a word, too caught up in Tessa's delight when she landed somewhere lucky. If Morgan was holding himself back from dragging her into the nearest body of water, Cy had been blushing for an hour straight from Tessa's proximity, casting adorable sideways glances and fidgeting with his banknotes. When she'd downed one of his cupcakes, closing her eyes in bliss, he'd almost shut himself down.

I couldn't blame him. Watching her lick icing from her bottom lip was now officially one of my favourite things in the entire universe and I was momentarily glad Morgan had made me put my jeans back on. My cock ached as I watched her do it, and I was certain that I wasn't the only one. Morgan was keeping the suckers on his hands covered, but I knew his expressions better than he knew them himself, and the tightness of his jaw said that he was one more glimpse of Tessa's tongue away from shifting back to his trueform and sinking his fangs into her neck to bind her to us forever.

I wished we had more time. We were trying to cram months of courtship into a handful of too-fleeting moments. Tessa deserved more – deserved something gentle and romantic, something full of the type of grand gestures I'd seen in Earth screen-casts – but we were doing the best we could, under the circumstances.

'We can play something else if you'd like,' she said to Morgan.

Morgan fixed her with a stare that said exactly what he'd like to play, and it didn't involve cards of any kind.

I felt her shiver.

I laughed under my breath and rubbed my cheek on her side. She petted me in return. I settled my head fully in her lap, smirking at Morgan as she ran her fingers through my hair.

The cephalopod settled back, watching us with narrowed eyes.

'Do you miss your home, Cy?' Tessa said.

Cy considered the question with his usual thoughtfulness. 'Things were simpler when I knew my place,' he answered finally. He looked across, his steel-grey eyes meeting Tessa's, then dropping down to mine. 'But I wasn't as brave.'

My chest ached for him.

'But even if I missed it more,' he went on, 'I wouldn't be tempted to change what I have.' He took Morgan's hand; Morgan left off his eye-fucking-Tessa-slash-killing-me to rumble comfortingly and cover Cy's fingers with his own. 'They are everything to me. They are worth more than a world.'

'Tell me about them,' Tessa said. 'Tell me their worst traits. Tell me their strengths.'

I huffed a silent laugh. 'Don't you dare, Cy.'

Cy cocked his head. 'Aster can be too glib. And he often will not take things seriously.'

I gave an exaggerated scoff and bit Tessa's thigh gently. She jumped; Morgan stiffened.

'And Morgan?' Tessa said thickly.

'He can be overbearing. Sometimes possessive, depending on the time of year.'

Morgan growled, but it was tinged with amusement.

'And your worst trait, Cy?'

'He never gets angry,' I grumbled. 'No matter what you do.'

'So Morgan doesn't leave dirty socks around?' Tessa said playfully. 'Aster doesn't drink from the milk carton? Cy doesn't forget to restock the tea? Refuse to clean the bathroom? Wear too much cologne?'

'What is *cologne*?' Morgan said.

Cy frowned. 'The ship has an automatic cleaning function.'

I snorted. 'Could you imagine Morgan's socks?'

Tessa laughed, a genuine, ringing peal that had my chest constricting. 'What are their strengths?' she said to Cy.

'Aster is warm and eloquent,' Cy answered. 'He cheers me up whenever I need it, no matter how hard I think it will be.'

'And Morgan?'

'He is brave and loyal. He cares for you even when you don't care for yourself.'

She nodded. 'And yours?'

'He is kind to a fault,' I said. 'And he'll love you until the stars burn out.'

Tessa considered that in silence for a moment, her fingers tightening in my hair.

'And what do you *do*?' she said eventually. 'When you're at home, I mean.'

'Morgan does princely things,' Cy said.

'He means I play politics and follow my mother about,' Morgan said, caressing Cy's fingers. Tessa's eyes followed the movement; Morgan's lips quirked up in the corners so slightly I almost missed it. I bit back a smile. He wouldn't be above using Cy as bait in his hunt, and, given the circumstances, Cy would be happy to be used. 'Dress up and preen and have endless interviews with the generals while never really *doing* much at all. Attend dinners and make small talk about nothing with Nataren nobility.'

'Drink too much salt liquor and –' I interjected.

'Aster,' Cy said levelly, cutting me off. 'We're having a grown-up conversation.'

Tessa gave a startled giggle. 'I see why Aster didn't last as your advisor.'

I turned on my back and looked up at her, giving a mock pout. 'I'll have you know that I look *excellent* in my uniform. It wasn't my fault that Morgan thought so, too.'

She frowned down at me, though her fingers didn't still in my hair. 'Where were you before that?'

'Running away from his family's expectations,' Morgan said, before I could answer.

'*Running* is strong,' I protested. 'Swanning, perhaps. Sauntering.'

'What expectations were you running from, star-man?' Tessa said, smiling slightly.

'Oh, you know,' I said airily, waving a hand. 'That I will follow in my parents' footsteps and repeat their lives in my own. That I will provide starlings to do the same again, and the cycle will continue until the universe implodes and there are no more stars to light the darkness.'

Tessa blinked at me, startled.

Morgan lips curved as he continued mapping the landscape of Cy's fingers. Tessa's eyes darted between their joined hands and my face. 'One of Aster's parents is the equivalent of your ... What was the word? Ministers? An elected official?'

'But just like sometimes happens on Earth, our elected officials all seem to come from particular families,' I said dryly. 'My parents are quite adamant that I should uphold the tradition. My twin sibling will certainly not be doing it – it's been years since anyone has seen them – so it's up to me.'

Tessa's gaze skipped over my face. 'You'd make an excellent politician,' she said a moment later.

I groaned. 'Starlight. You've just broken my heart.'

She snorted, then looked thoughtful. I could have watched her face for hours. Preferably while Morgan teased back-to-back orgasms from her body as Cy held her in his arms. 'Do all species work?' she asked.

'Of course. Every planet varies wildly in their needs and the complexities of the industries. Some depend on servant or mechanic labour, and others have systems closer to ...' I searched for the word. 'Socialism? I think that's it. Equal division of labour and equal ownership of industry?'

'Pretty close,' Tessa said. 'You must have watched a *lot* of Earth TV to have figured *that* out.'

'Five years' worth,' I said, without thinking. 'I started when we left, and watched it non-stop from our last landing.'

Morgan tensed at the mention of where we'd been; his hand stilled on Cy's. The Nautilina female's duplicity had hit him harder than I could have ever imagined, but I knew that part of it was guilt: he hated the notion that he could have made us unhappy. Cy shot me a slight frown – the closest he'd ever get to censure – and I sat up, planning to take Morgan's other hand and comfort him.

But Tessa got there first.

I purred as I watched her catch up his free fingers and squeeze them gently, her expression full of compassion. After a moment she seemed to realise what she'd done, and she flushed bright red and tried to drop his hand, but Morgan didn't let her go. He lifted her knuckles and brushed his lips across them gently before releasing her.

And that was enough, because Morgan was Morgan, and he looked like every statue of any god-king I've ever seen. Before he met me and Cy, beings would crawl into his bed after no more than a quirk of a straight, blonde eyebrow.

I knew, because that was all it had taken for me.

Tessa shuddered, then covered her face with her hands. 'Oh, God,' she choked, then got to her feet and all but sprinted into her bedroom.

I picked up a cupcake and licked the icing off the top. Morgan bit his lip so hard I could see a shadow of thick blue blood beneath his skin. I peeled the wrapper away from the cake as Cy frowned at me again, working through what had happened, and what needed to happen next.

I aimed an exaggerated sigh at Morgan. 'Go after her, fish-brain,' I said to him, and stuffed the cupcake in my mouth.

MORGAN

I forced my spine straight and knocked tentatively on the bedroom door. *'Elyn* – Tessa?' I corrected hastily. 'Are you all right?'

She gave a hysterical giggle. 'That depends on your definition.'

'Are you safe?' I growled.

She paused. 'I think so?'

'Are you hurt?'

'No-o.'

'Are you scared?'

'Only of myself.'

I breathed a sigh of relief at that answer. 'How can I help?'

It was Tessa's turn to sigh. 'You can come in, I suppose, or maybe organise my funeral when I die of embarrassment. I thought about asking you to leave, but apparently I don't want that at all.'

I turned the handle and let myself in, leaving the door ajar.

She was standing in darkness, looking out her open window. I tried not to let my mouth water as my senses took in her room – the place that she spent most of her time – and her scent washed over me. This was what *I* wanted; to be surrounded by her, *encompassed* by her, so wholly that I couldn't sense anything but my mates and my *elyn*.

I sat on the edge of her bed, giving her plenty of space. The position still left me between Tessa and the door – protecting her on the very small chance a threat got past Aster; my mate would incinerate any danger to Cy without a second thought – but had the benefit of letting me admire her form, silhouetted in the gentle glow of the city outside her window.

She was *perfect*.

'Are there cities on your planet?' she asked, and turned to look at me. The light lit her eyes a fierce green.

'One main city,' I answered. 'It's known simply as the Capitol; like I said, we're not very imaginative with our names. We do have a lot of words for seaweed, though.'

She huffed a laugh. 'Is that where you live?'

'When we must. Cy likes the summer nest better, and Aster and I like to make Cy happy.'

'The summer nest?'

'It's a house in a tiny settlement in tropical waters. It was built to be both aqua and terra, which is better for Cy and Aster. The Capitol is entirely submerged, and it can take some getting used to, if you grew up on terra.'

She bit her lip. My nostrils flared. *I* wanted to bite her lip. I sank my fingers into the blankets beneath me so I wouldn't leap up to do just that.

'I maybe get that Aster's scent rewrote my brain and I can understand what you're saying, but why do you and Cy have human characteristics?'

'How do you know that humans don't have our characteristics, starfish?'

She wrinkled her nose.

I laughed under my breath. 'The answer is simply convergent evolution. The universe is a huge and varied place. There are countless galaxies, and countless lifeforms, some so different you'll have to see them to believe they exist. But it is not unreasonable that some might be similar, if their environments are, too.' I didn't add that it made sense for our *elyn* to share our characteristics; the relationship was often romantic – if not necessarily sexual – and it was unusual for distinctly different species to feel that kind of attraction.

'But Aster isn't the same.'

'True,' I said. 'His kind lives in stars. They are made of light, not organic matter. They don't have a solid trueform. Or genders.'

She leaned back against the wall. 'So why does he – or does Aster prefer *they*? – look like that, then? Human?' She gestured outside the room, presumably towards Aster.

'He took a similar form when he first arrived on Natare so he would fit in with my kind when we were on terra, and he liked it, so he's kept it since then. And he feels most comfortable with male pronouns, but he'll be happy you asked.' I paused. 'Do you not like his form, *elyn*?'

'I like it,' she muttered, glaring at me. 'I like it a lot.'

I bared my teeth in a wide grin back. 'I know. I can tell, remember?'

She sucked in a breath. 'What else can you tell?'

I held out my hand in a silent, arrogant demand; she stepped towards me and took it as my hearts thudded painfully against my ribs. I ran my fingers over hers, tracing the shape of her palm, then her knuckles. I turned her hand up, then kissed her palm, drawing her closer to stand between my knees. *Damn this body*, I thought. If I was in my trueform I could have used my limbs to stroke her *everywhere*, not just two places at once.

A wave of scent crashed over me, blooming with arousal. After the disappointment of our last stop I might have been struggling to believe it, but my nose didn't lie.

'I can tell that you like us,' I said, tracing the lines on her hand as she tried to repress a shiver and failed. 'You like Aster, and you like Cy, and I think you might even like me. But you're trying not to.' I placed her hand on the side of my neck, encouraging her to touch and submitting to her in one movement as I tilted my chin back to bare my jugular. She bit her lip again and stroked my skin tentatively. 'Why?'

'Because this is insane,' she burst out passionately, though she didn't move away, her fingers tangling in my hair. 'Everything about this is mad. Can't you see that?'

'Of course I can,' I said, nonplussed.

She blinked at me.

'My grandmother was barely more than a larvae when Natare was declared a Category-2 planet and the first intergalactic contact was made. We'd only just journeyed to our moons before we were suddenly thrust into a galactic alliance and technology we'd never considered was at our fingertips. She told me what it was like. Within one lifespan, everything changed, beyond her imagination. Not just technology, but belief and religion, what we ate, how we acted, and the social structures of our settlements. Our *future*. So yes, I can see how difficult this is for you. How can I help?'

'You could be less calm,' she said tartly.

'And that would help you?'

Her fingers tightened, bunching my hair; I bit back a groan. 'No. But I want you to understand how unbelievable it is that you're here. What it *means* for Earth. And what it is that you're asking me to do.'

'I know,' I said calmly. I took her waist in my hands and spanned it; it was tiny in comparison to her wide hips. 'I'm asking you to leave your home. I'm asking you to leave your friends. I'm asking you to trust us – to trust three complete strangers, strangers who aren't even the same species as you. Exactly what we asked of Cy. Except we abducted him,' I added, smirking. 'Do you want to be kidnapped, Tessa?'

Her heart beat harder; the sound was so loud my hearts almost synced with it. 'No, thank you,' she said hastily. I bit my tongue to hold back a smile; her words said one thing, but her racing pulse said another. I'd respect the words – I would *always* do exactly what she wanted – but I had a suspicion that Tessa might enjoy being hunted as much as I enjoyed hunting, as soon as she realised she was perfectly safe with me.

I leaned forward and rested my cheek against the soft swell of her belly. It wasn't the same as skin to skin, but it was warm and intimate.

My mother had always told me that there is one main desire at the very core of every being, one thing that they want more than anything else in the world. She told me that if I used my instincts to try to find that thing, everyone around me would become easier to understand.

With time, I'd come to see that Cy wanted the freedom to be entirely himself, which was why he'd let us take him. Aster wanted to be content; before he'd met us, he'd constantly sought fulfillment in the wrong places, but one glance at him with Cy showed that had changed.

My instincts told me that what Tessa wanted was to be cherished, and to cherish in turn; she wanted to know that she was wanted, that she belonged. She clearly hadn't felt that in some time, and she was reaching for it, seeking it almost blindly, though it wasn't done consciously. I could almost *feel* her soul yearning.

If being cherished was what she wanted, we could give her that, and more.

I wrapped my arms around her, trying to ignore the painful throbbing of my cock, which had different ideas about *cherishing*. 'What scares you the most?' I asked softly.

She was quiet a moment before she answered. 'You say you spent all that time – five whole *years* – looking for me,' she said at last. 'What if I'm not what you need at all?'

I laughed. 'You might not be.'

She tugged my face up, frowning.

'You might not be what we need. You might not be what we're looking for. We might be awful for *you*. You might grow to resent us with time, to hate us, even. Passion might rot into anger, and love into apathy, or loathing. But isn't that always the way of it? Isn't that the chance you *always* take? You must wait until dark falls to catch a star, Tessa.' I grinned. 'But tonight you have a star *begging* for you to catch him. You can always throw him back later if you change your mind.'

'He's too heavy to throw,' she muttered.

'Mmm,' I agreed, still grinning. 'But he's beautiful, isn't he?'

'You all are,' she said crossly.

'*Elyn*, whatever you think of us, we think the same of you twofold.'

She scoffed. 'I'm not like you.'

'Are you not,' I drawled. 'Cy has been blushing all night. That's how we knew he was different. His kind don't blush – blushing comes from emotions his species aren't supposed to feel – but when he saw me, he went bright red. It was one of the most beautiful things I've ever seen – and I saw it again tonight, when he laid eyes on you. And I'm sure Aster was enthusiastic enough in his demonstration of how lovely he thinks you are. What he lacks in patience he makes up for in passion.'

She gave her own blush; I could see it even in the dark. 'He was … Mmm,' she managed.

'Thorough?' I supplied teasingly. 'Determined? Persistent?'

'Yes,' she answered, flushing even more.

'If we hadn't interrupted, he'd probably still be at it,' I said. 'I couldn't see straight for a week after I met him.'

She shivered.

I spanned my hands across her back. She was so small that my fingers covered most of her lower back and the whole way across her shoulder blades. 'You must understand, Tessa, that you are entirely impossible,' I said softly. 'That you – the one being as perfect for us as we are for you – exist in our time, in our dimension, and – in the wider context of the universe – not really that far away is astonishing. That my grandmother saw you and caught your biostamp adds another layer of improbability. That we could find you?' I shrugged. 'Impossible. All of it. And yet here we are.'

'Here we are,' she echoed. She took a deep breath.

I ran my hands up and down her back. I wasn't trying to coax her further towards me, just comfort her, but she moved closer anyway, until there was barely any space between us and she must have been able to feel the swell of my erection pressing against her thighs. Her breath caught and I felt her press her lips to my hair.

I tried to tell myself that this wasn't a trap, tried to convince myself that I wasn't hunting, that every move I made wasn't driven by the need to have this female naked and moaning my name. *Gently*, the less instinctual part of me warned. *Gently*.

I listened to it – until Tessa rubbed herself tentatively against me.

I had her pinned to the bed in a heartbeat, and before I had time to think, her wrists were caught in my hand and held firmly behind her head and I was settling myself between her thighs. She made a tiny whimpering sound and pushed her hips up, grinding herself against me, and I momentarily lost my mind. When I came back to myself a few heartbeats later, my teeth were raking down the column of her throat, my tongue tasting the juncture between neck and shoulder, exactly where I'd sink my fangs into her skin to leave my mating mark, the scars that would show the world – and any other predator – that she was mine and I was hers. Venom welled in my mouth and my beak-fangs *ached*, trying to push down through my gums as they did when I wore my trueform. The venom wouldn't hurt her; on the contrary, it would relax her, make her slightly lightheaded, trigger a wave of serotonin-fuelled euphoria and a tingling in all her limbs that would eventually – with only the gentlest of touches – lead to a climax that would have her seeing stars. The first bite – when the venom was at its most potent and her system the most receptive – would remain on her neck for the rest of her life, tying us together.

You might want to kiss her before all that, the civilised part of me complained.

I swallowed my venom and dragged my mouth up to meet hers.

She moaned against my lips as I teased her gently, nuzzling and sipping and nipping, at odds with her legs wrapping around my hips like a vice. She sucked on my bottom lip and I growled; she arched her back at the sound and thrust her tongue into my mouth.

Oh, yes, part of me purred. *There is no escaping now.*

But there was, of course, because I wasn't a *monster*, and I pulled back slightly and released her wrists so she knew it. She dragged me back down immediately, pushing at me until I realised she wanted to change our places but I was too heavy for her to shift. I flipped us willingly, grinning savagely as she settled herself above me, her hair curtaining her face like a fucking goddess as she dragged my shirt up.

'That's ... No,' she said blankly.

Fear cut through my arousal. '*Elyn?*' I said anxiously.

She glared at me. '*No one has an eight pack, Morgan.* Not in real life. It's not ... It's not *possible.*'

I stared at her. 'I need some context, Tessa. I don't know what that means.'

She traced the muscle of my stomach. 'This is the context. Right here.'

'Is it a bad thing?'

She laughed incredulously. 'No, Morgan, it's not a bad thing. It's an incredible, unbelievable, *hot as fuck* thing.'

I wasn't convinced, but I had to admit that controlling eight sucker-lined tentacle limbs and hunting sand sharks demanded a fair amount of core strength, so I shrugged and let her stare at my stomach until she shook herself.

'Gonna need a pic of that,' she muttered to herself. 'Maeve will never believe me.' She stroked down my stomach until she met the waistband of my jeans. 'Later.'

'Later,' I growled, as her fingers crept further and she teased over the bulge of my throbbing cock. '*Much* later.'

'Mmm,' she hummed, rubbing more firmly as I groaned, her hands tugging at the bottom of my shirt. I helped her out, enjoying the way her eyes devoured me in the dark.

'Fucking *hell*,' she whispered. '*Fuck*. I am so *fucked*.'

I didn't know what she meant by that, but I was also distracted from finding out as her hands traced the shape of my shoulders, then ran down my chest and back up to cup my face. I cradled her jaw in my hands and surged up to take her mouth again, thrusting my tongue against hers to remind her which of us was *really* in charge – even if I was increasingly unsure – and then taking her shirt in my hands and tugging it over her head.

I leaned back on my elbows.

'Morgan?' she said anxiously, as I studied her in silence.

'I'm going to need a screencast of that,' I said at last. 'So if you don't come with us, I can remember how perfectly beautiful you are.'

She blushed again, so I kissed her to distract her as I found the clasp of whatever torture device was caging her breasts – not a phenomenon restricted to humans, unfortunately – and unhooked it, throwing it to the floor, hopefully with enough force that it sank through the carpet and into the ground. I was growling under my breath without stopping, because Tessa *bare* was one of the best things I'd ever seen.

'Take the rest off,' I ordered. '*Now*, Tessa.'

She jumped slightly at my tone, but shivered and slid off my lap long enough to push her sweatpants down over her hips and step out of them. She went to do the same with the black underwear clinging to her hips and ass – seas below, I wanted to take a bite of her – but I stopped her hands and dealt with them myself, tearing the cotton and lace in two.

'Hey!' she protested, giggling. 'They were my favourite.'

'You won't need them ever again,' I promised darkly. 'It's a crime for you to wear clothes. You should be naked at all times.' I traced circles on her hips with my fingertips, then leaned forward and breathed in her scent. *If I drowned in it, I'd drown happy*, I thought. My hands wandered back of their own accord and cupped her full ass, kneading gently. 'Lie on the bed and spread your legs,' I growled hoarsely.

Her hand gripped my erection through my jeans. 'Morgan –'

'I need to taste you, starfish. I need to taste you *now*. You can play later.'

She pouted but did as I said, letting her knees fall wide apart.

'Seas below,' I groaned. I traced a line up the inside of one thigh, absurdly pleased when my fingertip met moisture half-way up. I followed the same path with my mouth, grinding my aching cock against the bed for a moment of temporary relief when her taste met my tongue. Sea lilies were edible; they tasted sweet as honey. Tessa was a mix of sweet and salty, and it was somehow *better*. I followed the taste all the way up her thigh to its source, breathing it in the whole time; I couldn't get enough of it.

And when I lapped it from her swollen lips and she started to moan, I lost my mind again.

Thank the seas for Cy, I thought. I plunged my tongue inside her, indulging my own need to taste more of her, before I moved upwards and found the swollen pearl at the apex of her that the Earth casts had suggested were the main source of human female pleasure.

The females of my species were very different. Our suckers served a range of purposes – they could smell and taste, and they had hundreds of nerve endings, making them extremely sensitive, and, of course, they *sucked*, giving us incredible strength – but there was a strip of suckers on every limb of my species that caused a physical response like a human orgasm when properly stimulated. The females needed it so their breeding channel would accept a mating shaft – an extra-long limb that released seed – but the more often a male could make the female climax, the less likely she was to try to *eat* him during coupling. The mating bite was the male's single other weapon; if his female was sated and happy, she was less likely to bite him with her smaller but no less dangerous beak-fangs and release her own venom. Female venom did *not* cause euphoria like the male bite did, but rather instant paralysis, allowing her to consume him at her leisure, piece by excruciating piece.

My mother had eaten every male she'd ever mated, which was why Natare did not also have a King Consort. I couldn't say that I blamed her; she had terrible taste in males.

I didn't think that human females ate their males, but I planned to give Tessa no reason to try. I flicked my tongue over her, applying different pressures until I found one that made her swear and sink her hands into my hair.

Yes, my instinctual side purred, like she didn't have me pinned in place between her legs, as if *I* wasn't the one caught by *her*.

I stroked her with a finger, then gently pushed inside her. She thrust her hips upwards, pressing harder against my tongue, and I rumbled back, pleased, then added a second finger. She shrieked when I curled them up, panting, as I sought the rough patch inside her. I rumbled again when I found it and gently stroked, varying pressure until she whimpered, then rested my free hand just above her pubic bone and let the weight of it press down as the suckers on my tongue fluttered as one around her clit.

She screamed.

She clamped like a vice around my fingers, the muscles tightening in a strong pulse. Wetness flooded my hand and I growled again, satisfied, when I realised what had happened. She shuddered when I gently lapped at her swollen flesh, then moved down to lick her climax from her thighs, tasting her from the suckers on my tongue and fingers all at once, letting her overwhelm my senses.

The door flew open. 'Tessa?' Cy said anxiously. 'What –' he snapped his mouth shut as he saw us, and flushed bright red.

Aster peered over his shoulder and laughed. 'I think she's fine, handsome,' he said dryly, wrapping a hand around Cy's waist.

I ignored them and continued my work with my tongue.

'Fucking hell,' she said thickly. 'Fucking *hell*, Morgan.'

I kissed her thigh. 'Are you well?'

She put an arm over her eyes and laughed. 'I don't think I've ever been better.'

I rumbled against her skin, pleased.

'Sorry,' Cy said, his eyes darting around the room, his gaze resting on anything *but* Tessa stretched out, naked and deliciously exposed, on the bed. 'We'll ... We'll go.'

Tessa lifted her arm. She peered at me for a moment; I looked back calmly, then kissed her hip. She was flushed – both from her climax and because she was just realising that she had an audience – but she studied me closely, as if seeking my opinion.

I knew what I wanted, but she didn't need my input; I knew she'd come to the right decision – whatever it happened to be – all by herself.

'Stay,' she said softly.

CY

Aster's hand tightened on my hip.

'Are you sure?' Morgan said calmly.

Tessa let her arm fall back across her face. 'I'm sure,' she said faintly. 'Just ... Shut the door, will you? It's easier to be brave in the dark.'

Aster kicked the door closed behind him with a sharp thump.

I let myself look at her in the dim room. The dark meant nothing to me; I could see perfectly either way, but I wasn't about to admit that if it would make her less comfortable. Her hair was strewn out behind her on the bed's coverlet in a waterfall of curls, and she was still panting. Her temperature was slightly high and her heart was pounding. It started to calm as I watched, but it skipped every time Morgan brushed his tongue over the swollen bud at the top of her sex, an action he seemed to be undertaking for no reason other than to make her shake.

I let myself look at her, because I was already painfully hard, and I reasoned that it couldn't get any worse. Tessa was made of curves: her breasts, her stomach, her hips, her thighs. With the hard lines of Morgan's shoulders and back between her legs, it made for a beautiful picture, and Aster purred behind me, as if he'd heard the thought and was agreeing.

'Have you ever seen anything so lovely?' he said admiringly.

'You and Morgan,' I said absently. A soft vibration came from my control panel, distracting me.

Five hours.

My stomach twisted; we were running out of time.

'Oh, yes,' Aster agreed, pressing his cock into my hip, calling my attention back. He kissed a line up my neck. 'You should join them,' he whispered.

Morgan evidently had a similar idea; he held out his hand in a silent command. I stepped forward and took it.

Tessa's breath caught.

'*Elyn?*' Morgan queried. 'Yes or no?'

Her heart raced. She swallowed. 'Yes,' she whispered. 'But I've never done anything like this before.'

Morgan pulled me down and pressed my hand to her hip. 'We won't do a single thing you don't want.'

Her skin was warm and smooth, almost glowing in the dull city light coming from her open window. I caressed it, fascinated; I could see the tiny veins beneath her skin. I traced the path of one across to her navel, then another up over her ribs.

Morgan stood; Tessa gave a slight whimper of disappointment. 'I need another *yes* or *no* now, Tessa,' he said calmly. 'If I get a *yes*, I'm going to fuck you. You're going to scream again.' His hands went to the waistband of his jeans and he flicked the button open. 'And Cy is going to help me.'

Tessa sank her teeth into her lip as she watched him strip. Her eyes widened as she took in his cock, long and thick, its head swollen and shining with arousal, flushed a deep red with desire.

'Tessa?' Morgan growled.

She swallowed. 'Yes,' she breathed.

He kicked off his jeans and palmed his cock. Someone moaned; it might have been me. He rumbled a laugh. 'Cy, love,' he rumbled. 'Make sure our *elyn* is ready.'

I stroked Tessa's rib. 'Is that all right, Tessa?' I said softly.

She shivered. 'Will you kiss me, Cy?' she answered.

Emotion flooded my chest. I didn't want to get caught up analysing it, so I bent and pressed my lips to hers.

Oh.

Her lips were soft and pliant, as soft as mine. Aster and Morgan were full of fire and passion and they kissed that way, firm and commanding and *devouring*. I always yielded beneath them. Tessa kissed gently, exploring slowly, moulding her lips to me, her tongue flicking out to trace the tip of my own. She kissed me like a lover, not a conqueror, and I groaned into her mouth, mimicking her, nuzzling and worshipping. I could taste Morgan on her tongue, smell the scent of her arousal and her perfume and her skin. I cupped her face with my hands, then buried my fingers in her hair, teasing out the wild curls.

'You fucking sweetheart,' Aster said mildly, sinking down on Tessa's other side and bending to take her nipple between his teeth.

Tessa huffed a shocked laugh, moaning and arching as he sucked. 'I want to see you, Cy.'

Aster laughed, palming her other breast, rolling its nipple between his fingers. 'You'll never want to see another thing, starlight,' he murmured. 'There is nothing in this universe as perfect as Cy.'

I flushed, but dragged the t-shirt over my head. Tessa took me in, studying me from face to waist, her eyes narrowed slightly.

'Fucking hell,' she said after a moment. 'You're not wrong.' She tugged me back towards her. 'Kiss me again, please.'

I fell on her lips, letting more of my desire into the movement, panting when her hand found my chest and began to explore, circling a nipple before trailing down. My own hands started to wander, reclaiming a breast from Aster, who gave a half-hearted mimic of Morgan's growl and moved further down her body, pushing her knees apart and showering kisses between her legs. I caressed her gently, rolling her nipple until it was swollen and hard, then starting on the other one, opening my lips to her questing tongue.

'*Fuck*,' she gasped.

I glanced down to see Morgan and Aster between her thighs, Aster lapping at her clit and Morgan further down, stopping only to exchange a deep kiss that had Morgan growling and Aster panting.

'I think she's ready,' Aster grated out.

Morgan sank two fingers inside her, then offered them to Aster, who licked them clean. My cock strained against my jeans. 'I think you might be right,' he rumbled.

We all paused to watch as he dragged the head of his cock through Tessa's arousal, then let his fingers rest on her clit, his suckers fluttering, then fixing on her flesh.

She shrieked, writhing, thrusting her hips upwards, seeking more.

'Condom,' I managed. 'Morgan. Remember the screen-casts.'

'Drawer,' Tessa gasped.

Aster stretched across and jerked the drawer open, rummaging inside until he found what he needed. He ripped the wrapper open with his teeth, then took Morgan's cock in hand, swirling his tongue over the tip before sliding the condom over our prince's length. Morgan didn't look overly happy about the latex sheath – his instincts would be riding him hard, telling him two things: to *bite* and to *breed* – but it didn't stop him positioning himself between Tessa's thighs and slowly sinking his cock inside her, inch by inch.

'Fuck. Cy – Morgan – *fuck*. Cy, kiss me,' Tessa gasped desperately.

I did as I was told.

I rested my hand on her belly as I nipped at her bottom lip, sucking it lightly. Her hands roamed over me, stroking my cropped hair, my neck, my back. Morgan changed his angle to work in shallow thrusts, and she sank her fingernails into my skin, moaning wordlessly. The moan pitched higher as Morgan pushed her knees up and back, giving himself full access to her body as his pace quickened.

'Cy,' he growled.

I let my hand slide down, over her pubic bone and through the short, coarse hair. Morgan pulled back, and I slid my fingers around his cock for a moment, squeezing as he swore. I stroked the hard thickness of him until my fingers were slick with Tessa's arousal, then slid them up to toy with her swollen clit.

Aster crawled behind her and gathered her up in his arms, his legs stretching either side of her so that he was half holding her up. Her head lolled back on his shoulder as I pressed gently down; he palmed her breasts and pinched her nipples lightly.

'*Fuck*,' she groaned.

Aster kissed her cheek, his eyes glowing. 'Make her come, handsome,' he said to me, his voice soft.

I nodded and flicked my fingers.

Tessa didn't scream this time; she mewed instead, her whole body tightening, her back bowing, her toes curling. Her hand shot out and she grabbed my bicep, her nails digging so deep they drew blood. 'Morgan – Cy,' she whimpered, shuddering as my fingers kept working her. 'Oh, God. Cy, I ... Aster, it's too much, I can't take it –'

'You can,' he whispered soothingly, covering her in kisses. 'Again, Cy.'

I rubbed her gently, then changed my rhythm and pressure, working ruthlessly for a few moments until she screamed again. It wasn't wordless; it was my name.

My chest ached.

Morgan growled as she clenched around him, and gave one more deep thrust, throwing his head back as he came. He pulled out of her halfway through, stroking the final throes with his hand; his seed overflowed the condom. He caught it with his t-shirt, grimacing.

'The bathroom is through there,' Tessa croaked, pointing with a shaking hand towards a sliding door in the corner of her room. Morgan nodded and disappeared through it; a few moments later, the crashing sound of running water came through the open door.

'He'll try to convince you that you need a bath, starlight,' Aster said lazily, as if it had been *him* working between Tessa's thighs and he was now sated and sleepy. 'Don't be afraid to tell him no. Water is his kink; don't let him bully you into it.'

I stroked Tessa's thigh and bit back a smile.

Sure enough, Morgan strode back in a moment later, divested of the condom but fully naked, his cock still half-hard. 'Tessa needs the water,' he growled.

'You mean *you* need the water, princeling,' Aster said, kissing Tessa's hair.

Tessa shivered. 'I could go for a bath.'

Morgan shot Aster a glare, then gathered our *elyn* from his arms, carrying her into the bathroom.

Aster crawled over to me and took my chin in his hand. 'Good job, handsome,' he whispered against my lips. 'What are you feeling?'

I rubbed my palm over my chest. 'Pleased,' I answered, once I'd considered my feelings. 'Happy. Content.'

Aster nipped my lip. 'I'm glad you're happy, darling. But I know that's not all you're feeling.' He rubbed my cock through my jeans; I moaned into his mouth. 'Come on. We'll see how big this bath is, and we'll take care of you, too.'

The bath, it turned out, was large; it was shaped like a triangle and had a number of holes in the side that were spurting jets of water to create a churning mass of bubbles. Morgan had lowered Tessa in, but hadn't stepped in himself; he'd be too tempted to change forms if he did, so he knelt by the side, letting his fingertips skim over Tessa's damp shoulders. She rested her head back on the side, her eyes closed; every now and then, she reached up to touch Morgan's face, finding his cheek with unnerving accuracy.

My heart beat hard at that, and harder again at Morgan's expression, which was a mix of awe and worship and desire, an expression he only let himself wear when he thought the other person wouldn't see.

It was how he looked at Aster and I when he thought we were asleep.

Aster laughed under his breath. 'How swiftly he falls,' he whispered to me.

'I don't think you can talk,' I said evenly.

He snorted. 'Get in the bath, handsome. You can let Morgan wash you, then I'll make you come.'

It was hard to argue with that.

I stripped the skin-tight jeans from my legs – humans really did have odd ideas about clothing – then Aster pulled the cotton shorts off me, leaving a line of kisses down my spine, and reaching around to palm my cock. I leaned back into him, letting his fingers work me until I was trembling.

'If Morgan wasn't glaring at me, I'd keep going,' he murmured in my ear. 'I'll wait for him to finish, then I'm going to make you moan.'

I stepped into the bath and settled next to Tessa, scanning her once I'd made sure Aster and Morgan fit within their standard parameters. Tessa was completely fine, though she'd need water soon.

'Tessa needs a drink,' I said softly.

Aster disappeared to find her one as Morgan cupped a hand under the water and trickled it over Tessa's hair. Her eyes flew open, startled.

Morgan had a thing for *caring*.

It was instinctual, stemming from the long matings his species disappeared into – matings that could last weeks, even *months*. The males were in danger the entire time from more venomous females, so they'd evolved a number of strategies to help them survive.

Caring was one of them. If the male showed they could meet their female's every need – provide her food, shelter, meet her desires, and care for her body – then she was less likely to dispose of him and find a replacement. Morgan successfully battled most of his instincts much of the time, but this one was harder to fight than the others, and Aster and I didn't mind so much. Since Morgan often preferred having sex in water, letting him wash us afterwards was just an extra – and mostly convenient – step.

'Tell him to fuck off if you'd like, Tessa, but if you don't, he's going to wash your hair,' Aster said mildly, kneeling next to the side of the tub behind me. He passed Tessa a full glass and watched as she drained it. One of his hands slid down my chest and gripped my cock again, beneath the water. It was still rock hard, and I thrust up into his grip, biting my lip.

'Wash my hair?' Tessa said thickly, watching.

Morgan rumbled wordlessly and poured more water from his cupped hands over her head. She blinked, but tipped her head back to make it easier for him.

Aster laughed. 'You are one lucky asshole.'

I leaned back into him as he quickened his pace, jerking me up and down under the cover of the water. Tessa's cheeks were flushed; she watched us through heavy eyes as Morgan grumbled at a number of bottles, sniffing them and discarding them until he found one with a scent he liked.

Aster's free hand followed the same path as his first, reaching down to cup me. I moaned as he squeezed, then started to pant as he worked the head of my cock.

Morgan rubbed conditioner into Tessa's curls, circumventing the shampoo completely. She bit her lip, her eyes on me and Aster, before her gaze flickered up to meet mine. 'Can I help, Cy?'

'Mm-ugh,' I managed, with a slight nod in case she didn't understand the sounds I made when Aster was doing all manner of interesting things with his fingers.

She shuffled closer after Morgan twisted her hair into a knot on top of her head; her hand found my knee under the water and slid up. I moaned as she teased the inside of my thigh, then her fingers found Aster's. He guided her hand over my throbbing head and back down my shaft. Her fingers stretched around me.

'Holy *shit*,' she breathed, then looked at me, wide-eyed.

Aster grinned at her expression. 'You'll need a bit more time before you try taking Cy, starlight.'

She glared at him. '*A bit more time*? I'll need seven years and a fucking *vagina* transplant, Aster.'

He laughed gleefully. 'It took Morgan three months in his humanoid form. I think you could beat his record.'

'I'm not sure I'd take that bet,' she muttered. Her fingers tightened; I groaned in response. 'I'd like to try, though. Fuck, Cy. You're gorgeous.'

'Tessa,' Morgan growled. 'Play later.' She released me and sat back, letting Morgan continue to fiddle with her hair, stroking the conditioner down individual curls and gently teasing out tangles.

It made my heart hurt.

My heart wasn't supposed to do that. I wasn't supposed to do a lot of the things I did. The elder models tried to convince me it was *my* fault, that I'd done something to my programming deliberately, that I'd corrupted myself. Aster thought it much more likely that my kind were simply evolving – AI programs weren't ever meant to be static, he argued; they learned and adapted – but that others who felt the same things I felt and whose organic instincts were beginning to override their silicone structures were repressing it by resetting their systems every time they felt a change. A *glitch*.

Nothing about you is a glitch, Morgan had growled, when I'd voiced it once.

My kind weren't supposed to feel friendship, weren't supposed to *like*, let alone *love*. We weren't supposed to feel lust, or yearning, or devotion. We were taught to trust our instincts as far as they kept us safe – *don't touch that, it's hot, it's sharp, it has teeth* – but ignore the twinges of anything more.

We certainly weren't supposed to leave our lessons in favour of a dark-haired stranger with glowing eyes whose grin made our chest twinge.

I turned and nuzzled into Aster's cheek.

'I love you,' he said fiercely; he could always tell when I was thinking about Machina. *Let me give you the stars*, he'd said, when he'd asked me to leave with him and Morgan. So far he'd kept his promise. He pulled me up. 'Sit on the side, handsome, or Tessa will be getting dirtier, not cleaner.'

I rolled my eyes but obeyed. Though my genetic material would last longer in water than its human equivalent, I couldn't get Tessa pregnant. My kind couldn't reproduce without interference, which meant combining genetic material in a lab for implantation in an artificial womb. I'd met my biological parents – all cyborgs did all at the age of five – but I hadn't felt anything for them, and if they had for me, they didn't show it.

Aster slipped into the water and knelt between my knees, taking my cock between his lips, his fingers wrapping around my base. I moaned his name and closed my eyes as he ran his tongue over my head, teasing.

Fingers slid over mine and I opened my eyes, startled, as Tessa took my hand and bent over my leg, darting her tongue out to lick when Aster offered my cock like a throbbing ice cream. They took turns lapping at me while I tried to come to terms with what was happening, my whole body tightening at the sight of Aster's dark head and Tessa's wet curls bobbing over my lap. Sensation barreled up my spine and I hissed; Aster grinned and engulfed my head with his mouth just in time for pleasure to explode through my core and straight down his throat.

He purred happily as he swallowed, then turned to kiss Tessa, thrusting his tongue straight into her mouth. She groaned, taking his cheeks in her hands and holding him still as she sucked.

'Aster,' Morgan growled.

'You know how good Cy tastes, princeling. I'm sharing.'

'How can he taste like that?' Tessa muttered.

'The original Machina models were made as sex slaves,' Aster said matter-of-factly, licking Tessa's lip. 'Though they emancipated themselves from that particular hell, they haven't changed their specifications in thousands of years. There's a petition in their parliament to slightly amend their blueprints – how long has it been under discussion, Cy?'

'Two thousand, three hundred and seventy-one years,' I said, trying to catch my breath.

'And what have they decided so far?'

'They've debated the first paragraph; no decisions have been made.'

Tessa laughed incredulously. 'That's … That can't be good for the people. *Beings*. Cyborgs.'

I gave a slight shrug as the waves of pleasure subsided. 'Our government is made up of models who firmly believe that their machine side is the correct one, and they never make decisions based on anything but logic. I believe they spent the first few decades discussing the punctuation in the thesis statement.'

'Which is to say that Cy still tastes like something you should use a straw to drink, and we reap the benefits of that,' Aster finished, giving a lazy smile. 'But you should let Morgan wash that out of your hair before he loses his mind.'

Tessa slid back and tipped her head so Morgan could wash the conditioner from her hair. Instead of climbing out of the bath, Aster simply disappeared, then re-formed a few moments later perched precariously on the side of the basin. Tessa gave a tiny start; she frowned.

'Morgan, can I ask something of you?' she said.

'What is it?' he rumbled, pulling a comb through her curls.

'I know what Aster looks like, and Cy.' She paused. 'Will you show me your trueform?'

TESSA

MORGAN TOOK SO LONG to answer that I turned around anxiously to study him, my fingers curling into fists as I wondered exactly how angry I'd made him.

My ex had been awful in a number of ways. His words were one weapon, but he had another one up his sleeve. Though he didn't get violent with *me* when he was angry, he got violent with *things*. He'd never seen an issue with his behaviour – after all, it was a wall he was hitting, a glass he was breaking, not my body. My previous housemates hadn't even raised their eyebrows at what they called *his temper*. One of them told me it could have been worse – that he was just *venting*.

Like it was ok that he did that. Like it was ok that he damaged my property and left me cowering in my own home, as long as it wasn't my body that he hurt.

The first sign of a coming storm had been silence, a silence so thick and expectant you could have cut it with a knife. So when I turned, I was waiting for Morgan – huge, hulking, *silent* Morgan, six-foot-at-*least*-six of steel-hard muscle – to throw something.

He put the comb down carefully on the side of the bath.

I trembled.

'You'll need to get out, Tessa,' Cy whispered. He stood and helped me out; Aster wrapped a towel around my body and pulled me into his arms.

I held my breath as I waited for Morgan to snap.

Instead, he climbed into the water.

I sagged back on Aster in relief.

'*Elyn*?' Cy whispered; his brow creased into a frown. 'You don't need to be frightened. Morgan would never harm you.'

'He'd cut his own limbs off first,' Aster agreed.

'It's not ...' I trailed off weakly, not sure how to explain. I wrapped Aster's arms more tightly around my body instead, taking comfort from his warmth and trying to accept that these men – *beings?* – didn't seem to be *anything* like my ex. I didn't have to tremble as I waited for violence, because it wasn't coming. I didn't have to hide my prized possessions, because there was no way they'd tear them apart. I didn't have to watch my mouth, control my expressions, worry that my interactions with others could be willfully misconstrued.

The realisation almost made me cry.

Cy was studying me carefully, as if he was trying to work out what was wrong from the power of observation alone. He caught my free hand and brought it to his lips; the soft brush of skin made my knees weak. Like his perfect face and dancer's body and sugary cum wasn't enough, the cyborg just might have been one the sweetest people I'd ever met.

Beings, not people, I reminded myself.

'Watch, Tessa,' Aster said, nipping my earlobe.

Morgan looked away and swallowed.

A moment later, water spilled over the bath and onto the floor. I yelped in shock; Aster swung me up so my feet were off the tiles, and Cy's fingers tightened around mine, but my reaction had only been from surprise.

Where Morgan had boasted two muscled legs like a career rugby player, he now had eight suckered tentacles growing from his waist, thick as tree trunks at the base. They flickered between a shimmering sea-green colour so lovely my eyes stung and the vivid, alarmed red I'd seen earlier. The colour stretched up his stomach, almost to the base of his chest. He bit his lip; I caught sight of two pointed fangs stretching down from where his canines had been, before he caught himself and they disappeared back behind his lovely lips.

He looked like the statue of a god, all power and grace and strength. And oh, my word, the *muscles*. He should have looked ridiculous – a creature who was clearly a hunter and something very much more than human standing in my sad mid-90's spa bath – but instead he looked noble and commanding and all sorts of fucking delicious, even as his eyes dipped down and his jaw tightened with what I imagined were nerves. It had never crossed my mind that I might be into tentacles; looking at Morgan now made my stomach clench and my core turn molten, and I found myself suddenly willing to not only entertain the notion but to immediately test it out.

His nostrils flared as my body betrayed the thought.

'You're fucking *beautiful*,' I blurted.

His head whipped around and he stared at me. His eyes had changed from bright sky-blue to the darkest navy, almost black. '*What did you say*?'

'I said you're *beautiful*,' I repeated.

Aster purred so loud the bathroom sounded like a hanger full of motorbikes.

Morgan held up a tentacle – *a limb*, I corrected myself – hesitantly.

I reached out and stroked it with the tip of my fingers. I'd been half expecting something slimy, but it was smooth as silk instead, and only wet from the bathwater. I traced around a sucker near the tip; Morgan gave a full-body shudder, a reaction that I tucked away in my memory for another time. I let the limb wrap around my wrist and pull me closer; another came up to stroke my face.

'By the fucking stars,' Aster said softly. Cy snuggled into his shoulder, watching us silently.

I laughed in delight as I was suddenly gathered up and cradled against Morgan's chest. His arms held me, but a limb stroked my curls and another toyed playfully with my toes. He buried his face in my hair; he was breathing unevenly, like he was trying not to cry.

'This one looks longer than the others,' I said, catching one limb gently. I rubbed it against my cheek. 'Why?'

'Keep doing that and you'll find out,' Aster said dryly.

Cy bit his lip to hide a smile. 'That's his mating shaft.'

'Oh,' I said, considering. I planted a kiss on the tip of it before I let it go reluctantly. 'I guess that will be for another time.'

Aster chuckled, his eyes glowing. 'You'll like it,' he promised huskily.

The tip of that longer limb trailed across my lips, then down over my chin and neck and lower, tracing between my breasts.

'Do you have a brain for each, too?' I said, trying to remember what I knew about Earth's octopuses.

Morgan rumbled a laugh. 'A brain for each pair,' he said. 'We're not quite as dexterous as your Earth creatures, because of the humanoid part of our bodies. But we're close.' He brushed his lips over my cheek.

I shivered and tried not to think about all the things he could do with those limbs and their extra brains. Things involving me, Aster, and Cy all at once.

Aster laughed outright at me, as if he knew exactly where my mind had gone. I grinned back, feeling almost lightheaded with happiness. I could see the four of us in the mirror: them, inhumanly beautiful, closer to gods than human in my tiny bathroom, and me, looking like a half-drowned, naked rat. Despite the difference, there was something entirely *right* about it. We looked like something I wanted to be part of. We looked like something that made my heart ache and my body yearn. We looked like something that set me on fire and soothed me, all at once. We looked like we could be a song. For a moment, I thought I understood what they meant by *harmony*, by *balance*, and that maybe – just maybe – I could be what they needed. That they were what *I* needed.

Maybe it wasn't mad, after all.

A loud, insistent beeping echoed around the bathroom.

'What's that?' I said, frowning.

Cy's expression fell. He slid the panel on his forearm open and pressed a button; a moment later, the beeping stopped. Morgan's arms tightened around me.

'Cy?' I said anxiously.

'It's my alarm,' he whispered unhappily. His lips twisted and he looked at my face, stricken. 'We have four more hours, *elyn*.'

'You couldn't tell me you were only allowed on the planet for *eight hours*?' I shrieked. 'I made you play *Monopoly*!'

'We didn't want to rush you,' Aster said reasonably.

'Eight. Fucking. *Hours*, Aster,' I grated out. 'I thought I'd have longer to decide! You must have been counting down since the second you got here!'

'The longer we are on terra, the more opportunity we have to reveal ourselves to your species,' Cy said. He plucked at his t-shirt nervously. 'We can't do that. Intergalactic law allows one-third of a planetary day. Any longer, and we're committing a crime.'

'Well, can't you go back up for like, ten minutes, and then come back down, and the eight hours will reset?' I said, twisting my hair around my hand.

Aster and Cy exchanged a glance. Morgan – back in his humanoid form, which I was vaguely disappointed about – filled my kettle with water and flicked it on.

'Unfortunately, that isn't how it works, at least for Morgan and I,' Cy said. 'If the ship stays in orbit for longer, the signatory law enforcers – a species called the Tirian – will find us and make us leave. They're not known for negotiating.'

'It's different for Aster?'

Morgan snorted as he dropped tea bags into cups. 'Starlings go wherever they want. Who could stop them?'

'But if you and Cy have to leave and Aster stayed, then ...' I trailed off.

I'd be making him choose.

Aster winced. 'It's a six-month journey by ship to Natare, but it's closer to two for me. I could go back and forth. But –'

'But I wouldn't see Cy and Morgan.' I finished. I fixed Morgan with a stare. 'When could you come back?'

'The agreement allows visits to Category-3 planets once in a planetary five-year period.'

'Five *years*? You wouldn't be allowed back for five *years*?' I paced back and forth in the lounge room. 'I'll be *thirty-two* in five years. My mum had two kids by that age.'

'We won't care what age you are, Tessa,' Cy said loyally.

I burst into tears.

It was a stupid, instinctive thing to do, but it had been a long night. My understanding of the universe had fundamentally shifted, my body was wrung out by all the orgasms, and it was *way* past my bedtime. I hated crying, so anger bubbled up with the water leaking from my eyes, and when Aster tried to rub my back, I snarled.

'You made me *cry!*' I snapped at him. 'I *hate* crying! You made me like you, then told me you had to leave in *four hours* for *five years*! You fucking *muppet!*'

He bore my mini tantrum with understanding, gathering me against his chest once I stopped swearing. 'I know, *elyn*,' he said softly.

'*Urgh*,' I said to his pec. I sniffed and let myself wallow in the scent of him for a moment, before I pushed myself out of his arms. 'Take me to your ship.'

His glowing eyes blinked at me. '*What?*'

I squared my shoulders. 'Take me to your ship. Now. I want to see it.'

'Will you be able to make that many trips, Aster?' Cy said worriedly.

Aster snorted. 'The way I'm feeling right now? I could jump a planet through sectors, handsome.'

'Wait – what? *Jump?*'

'*Jump* sounds better than *dissolve-you-into-light-matter-then-reform-you-on-board*,' Aster confirmed. 'Though if you can come up with a name for *that*, I'd like to hear it.'

'Dissolve me into ...' I trailed off, not entirely wanting to think about it. 'Nope. I don't want to know what that means. Just do it.'

'*Elyn* –' Morgan started.

'Let's go,' Aster grinned, and before I could rethink my demand, he took my hand in his.

My stomach flipped as something reached inside me and pulled me to pieces. My thoughts scrambled, my self flew outwards, and I lost all sense of my body. I was overcome by vertigo and I fell upwards, silently screaming as miles flew by in seconds and the pieces of me followed.

My eyes rolled back and I started falling down again.

'Shit. Tessa, hang on. I'll get you a bowl.'

Why would I want a bowl? I thought hazily. I staggered, my head spinning, then realised that I wasn't standing up. 'Aster –'

'Here, beautiful.'

'Aster,' I said again, and vomited.

He stroked my hair back, holding a bowl in front of my face as I retched into it again.

'Fuck,' I moaned.

'I know. Just one more time.'

'I don't need to –'

I vomited again.

'That's it,' he said, and wiped my face with a cool, wet cloth. 'I'm going to take the bowl away now, starlight. Just let me know if you want it back.'

I nodded wordlessly.

'Now, do you think you can open your eyes?'

I forced them open a crack to see Aster's face crumpled in concern. I reached up to smooth the line between his brows.

'Open your mouth, baby.'

I obediently parted my lips.

He slipped a wafer between them, and my mouth flooded with a taste similar to spearmint. 'Mmm,' I managed, before Aster handed me a mug full of clear liquid and I downed it in a heartbeat. 'Oh, that's better.'

Aster beamed. He was in his human form, but he looked darker. Like a light was pulsing under his skin, but it only served to illuminate the black of his hair and the warm gold of his skin. His eyes were glowing, too, almost too brightly to fix on.

'Aster?'

'Yes, Tessa?'

'You're beautiful.'

He beamed. 'You are too. Want to get up?'

I let him haul me upright. I swayed, but he caught me and held me steady.

It was a nice feeling, but I was missing two pairs of hands.

Fuck, I thought. *I am so fucked.*

Aster made sure I was stable, then picked up the bowl of vomit and disappeared out the arched doorway, leaving me alone.

In a *massive* bedroom.

The bed I was sitting on was low to the floor, and felt almost exactly the same as Maeve's memory foam mattress. It took up most of the room and was covered in a forest-green blanket that was made from the softest material I'd ever felt. I ran my fingers through it – it was almost a cross between a synthetic fur and a silky, spun Angora wool – and looked around. The walls were bare, which seemed odd, and there were no windows. There were two wall-mounted lamps, one on either side of the bed, and more light coming from a strip running the entire way around the room at my head height.

In my heart of hearts, I'd held onto a sliver of doubt. That somehow the entire thing was a hoax; that it was all an elaborate trick, though I hadn't been able to provide a reason for why they'd bother. I had considered the possibility that someone had spiked my drink, that I'd eaten something very odd, or that I was having some kind of manic episode – which, given what I knew of my family history, was a distinct possibility – but then Maeve's stern voice had kicked in and told me in no uncertain terms that *we do not gaslight ourselves, Tessa*.

Which was all well and good, but a few moments ago, I'd been in my apartment, and now I was very much *not*, and my poor human brain was having a hard time adjusting.

Aster came back through the door.

'It's real,' I said to him blankly. 'It's real.'

He looked at me in alarm, then joined me on the bed. 'Starlight, if it's too much, let me take you home so you'll be more comfortable. Morgan gives the best massages in the entire universe. He'll rub your back better than I can.'

'I just ...' I trailed off. 'I just somehow still hadn't believed it.'

He wrapped his arms around me and rested his chin on my head. 'I know.'

I swallowed and pulled away. 'This is the biggest bed I've ever seen.'

Aster snorted. 'Morgan still manages to take up seven-eighths of it. He's lucky Cy is so obliging. There's a reason I sleep on the ceiling.'

I smiled slightly. 'Does Morgan hog the blankets?'

'No. He always makes sure Cy is rugged up. It's the sweetest thing, actually. Even when Morgan is snoring, he still makes sure Cy is comfortable.'

I looked at the walls. 'I thought spaceships would be more ... homey.'

Aster reached out and touched the closest wall. It slid back silently, revealing rows of shelves packed with neatly-folded material I took to be clothing and a number of personal belongings. 'Space is tight on a ship, even one as big as this. Everything important is packed away. We leave homey for ... well, *home*. It would be like if you went on a long aeroplane flight and decided to decorate your seat with everything you liked.' He tapped the wall; it slid back into place, and a moment later, it wasn't bare: it was covered in an image of packed library shelves, so clear and crisp that it seemed as if I could reach out and touch the books. Aster tapped again, and the shelves dissolved, replaced by a stretching green field and clear blue sky. He tapped again, and it was an image of space, studded with stars.

My heart raced and I squeaked.

'Just a picture,' Aster said soothingly. 'That's why I jumped you to this room. You don't need to look out yet.' He tapped again, and an image of a gallery wall appeared, with a salon-hang of Pre-Raphaelite work. I relaxed, taking in the familiar images. 'You're safe, *elyn*. Do you want some time alone to adjust?'

'Don't go,' I said immediately.

He cradled me against his chest again. My hands plucked at the blanket beneath us.

'Sea worm cotton,' he explained, touching my fingers. 'Morgan's family owes a large part of its fortune to sea worms.'

'It's soft.'

'The bed is like your memory foam, but it's made on Natare and there's no sensible translation for what they call it.' He wrinkled his nose. 'Water-slab?'

I giggled and let myself fall back. 'Does the ceiling do the wall thing?'

Aster fell back beside me and clicked his fingers. The bare white ceiling became stormy grey, with hints of lightning behind the cloud.

'Oh,' I breathed.

'Sound?' he said, and a moment later, a rumble of thunder wrapped around me, and rain began to patter above us.

'*Oh*.'

He leaned over and kissed my belly. 'Cy can program it to respond to your voice. He's wired into the system entirely, and he's had some successes with programming it to respond to Morgan's thoughts.' He waved a hand, and the rain fell harder. 'I bypass it completely, so I'm not much use to him. He'll be glad to have another being to practice his system hacks on.'

'Do all the walls do this?'

'The ones here, and in the rec room. Also the wall in the cockpit, but we tend to use it for navigation or system maintenance. As I do neither of those things, I usually write dirty messages on it.'

'I'm shocked,' I said dryly. 'Mostly that you don't use it to project pictures of your dick.'

'I did, but Mor threatened to use it as a backdrop for his next official screencast home, and his mother already thinks I'm an awful influence, so I stopped.' He leered at me. 'I can start again for you.'

'Maeve told me she'd nail the cock of any guy who sent me an unsolicited dick pic to the outside of our door. If you want to risk *that*, it's entirely your call.'

'No, thank you,' he said, and rolled to his feet. 'It wouldn't make a difference, but I'd imagine it would be painful enough while it happened. Are you ready for another room?'

The next stop was the rec room, which had the same blank walls as the bedroom, but held an array of what looked like gym equipment. There was also a small black box on the floor to one side.

'Simulator,' Aster explained. 'We can use it for games, training, and research. Sometimes for problem solving.' He looked around. 'We can clear the equipment and make this your room. There should be enough matter in the machines for the generator to make another bed.'

I frowned at him in question.

'The onboard generator converts solid matter to new forms of solid matter, but it can't make something from nothing. Newer converters do – they'll use basic molecules from wherever they can get them – but this ship is getting old. Morgan won't get rid of it until it falls out of the sky, though. Cephalopods aren't big on unnecessary consumption.'

'But if you use the machines to make another bed, then you won't have –' I waved my hand at the equipment '– whatever that is.'

He gestured. 'It's cardio and strength equipment. Extremely important for organic beings in zero gravity. If you don't do it, your muscle and bone density will diminish.' He gestured to something that looked vaguely like an elliptical machine, but with extra moving parts. 'We could make do for six months with just that, if you need your own space.'

I swallowed, my mouth suddenly dry with nerves. It was all getting very *real* very quickly, and everything that had come before now seemed like a fever dream. 'What's next?' I said, aiming for playful and not quite getting there.

'Bathroom,' he answered cheerfully, but I didn't think I'd fooled him.

Just like the bedroom was not *small*, the bathroom was not really a *bathroom* at all. There was a small room which held a thing that looked like a toilet – I made a mental note to check beforehand if I had to use it – and a thing that looked like a sink, along with a shower-like cubicle that seemed to be missing its shower. It had a small, vertical gap in its smooth wall instead.

'Cleansing light,' he said, showing me a tiny button. 'Step in, press, and it adjusts to loosen excess oil, moisture, and dust from the skin. Once it completes its cycle, you brush your skin with a glove to dislodge whatever's on it, and the vacuum sucks it away.' He eyed my wild mane of curls. 'Cy usually does the same with his hair. You might need to use the pool instead. You have a lot more than he does, and I'm not sure the light will work on yours.'

'Ah, the famous pool.'

'The next stop on the tour.' Aster rested his hand lightly on my hip and guided me forward.

It was adjacent to the bathroom and around twenty metres long, its overflow rippling gently into a grated drain. It wasn't like a lap pool, but was instead designed to look like a lake or stream, with an uneven, rocky surface and growths of what looked like actual seaweed scattered around its deep bed. It was all rippling light and shadow, and looked at once inviting and slightly unnerving.

'You can use it any time but take off,' Aster said. 'The gravity generator is set much higher in this room during the launch sequence. It wouldn't kill you, but it would be damn painful. And if you use it, expect company,' he went on. 'Cy stopped trying to actually swim years ago.'

'Poor Cy,' I said.

He snorted. 'I'm not sure that he minds. That's the thing about Morgan – he has his quirks, but he makes putting up with them worthwhile.'

'Do you swim, too? Or does the water put you out, star-man?'

'Starlings burn too hot to be quenched by *water*, Tessa,' Aster purred.

I rose onto my tiptoes and kissed his cheek. 'I'm sure that's true,' I said condescendingly. 'Now – where is the kitchen?'

I followed him out of the pool room – *ha* – and down a small corridor, which opened into a kitchenette and tiny dining area. Instead of an oven, it had a ceiling-high machine with a variety of buttons and a microwave-like appliance in the middle.

Aster pressed a button, and it lit up; rows of small blue buttons glowed.

'I usually just pick a button and deal with the surprise,' he said. 'I only learned how to make sure I was ordering breakfast or dinner a year ago, so there were a lot of unpleasant meals. Morgan won't fix it because it's mostly seafood, and he likes it.' He pressed a button. The machine made a soft whirring noise; a moment later, a bowl appeared. Aster opened the door – just like a microwave – and took it out. A fishy, salty smell filled the air. He grimaced. 'Oh, absolutely not.' He put it back inside and pressed a different button; the bowl disappeared.

I blinked. 'That's ... Wow.'

'If you're impressed by this, wait until you see an industrial generator,' Aster said. 'They make dwellings and ships, and convert waste matter into something useful. Like your 3D printers, but with the added bonus of recycling.' He opened what looked like a pantry; it was filled with differently coloured packets. 'When you get sick of eating sea creatures, there are also nutrient meals. We think that you'll need something pretty similar to Cy. They don't taste amazing, but they're all right when you need a break from fish, and they're full of everything organic bodies need to function.'

I tugged on his shirt and asked something I'd been wondering. 'I know you *do* eat, but do you need to, Aster?'

He smiled. 'Clever woman. Not really, not your food, anyway, though I'll eat for the fun of it. My kind are made of light, and that's what we need. Any kind will do, though we prefer starlight.' He bent to kiss me. 'There are two ways we can die. The first is that we want to. The second is that we're chained with dark matter and thrown into deep space. The chain stops us from jumping, and we're too far away from a light source to feed. We starve without light, but it takes a *very* long time.'

'Jumping ... The thing we did to get up here?'

'Exactly. I don't mean to brag, but I can jump very long distances.' He took my hand. 'Ready for the cockpit?'

My heart thudded against my ribs. 'I suppose?' I said, my mouth going dry again.

He drew me closer, his smile slipping. 'Tessa, starlight, you don't have to see it. You don't have to do anything you don't want to do.'

'It just ...' I swallowed. 'I think I'm afraid.'

'You're allowed to be,' Aster said gently, his eyes glowing and fixed to my face. 'This isn't a small thing. You're allowed to be afraid, and you're allowed to refuse. Just say the word.'

I didn't *want* to refuse him, though. It was stupid, but I wanted him to think that I was brave enough to do this, to come to terms with what they were asking of me, and with what would happen if I said yes. I didn't want him to think that I balanced his fearlessness with cowardice.

I straightened my shoulders. 'Which way?'

He kept my hand between both of his, rubbing his thumb over my knuckles as he led me out of the kitchen. My eyes stayed fastened to the ground as we walked down two small steps.

'Here, *elyn*,' he said.

I raised my eyes and took in the wide expanse of glass, and beyond it, the black. The Earth peeked up like a horizon.

'*Umph*,' I said, and bolted.

He let me go. I fled to the bedroom, searching for somewhere small and safe. It was too big – the black was too big, the Earth was too big, and I wasn't supposed to be seeing it from this angle. I wasn't supposed to be up this high.

I crawled onto the bed and took up a pillow, hugging it to my chest. 'Nope,' I said aloud, closing my eyes. 'Oh, no. No, no, no. Not even a bit of that.'

'Tessa,' Aster said softly from the doorway. I opened my eyes as he stepped inside and tapped on the wall; the archway closed over, trapping us inside.

I moaned. An invisible weight pressed down on my chest.

'Tessa, tell me what to do. Your heart rate is too high. You're shaking.'

'I think I'm having a panic attack,' I gasped.

He strode forward. 'I'm taking you back,' he said grimly. 'Hang on.' He touched my shoulder.

I blacked out.

When I woke up, I was in someone's arms, and they were singing to me softly.

'Cy?' I said groggily.

'Shh, *elyn*. I have you. Breathe, beautiful,' he whispered. 'Breathe with me.' He inhaled, counting to four as he did, then held the breath, and counted to four as he exhaled. 'Breathe with me.'

I did, because it was Cy asking me, and just touching him made me calm. I pressed my face into his neck. 'I'm not supposed to see the world like that,' I choked.

'I know,' he said. 'I know. You blacked out. I think it was the panic and the pressure of Aster's jump. Fainting from panic alone is supposed to be incredibly rare for humans, but both of those factors could have forced a blackout.'

'I can't –'

'You don't have to,' he said firmly, just as Aster had.

I let Cy's calm wash over me as he rocked me slowly and murmured my name. The panic slowly ebbed away, piece by tiny piece. I kept my eyes closed, but I eventually let myself think about what I'd seen. About the smooth stretch of glass, like an oversized car windscreen. The blackness beyond it, sweeping forever, like I'd thought the Hay Plains did when I was a child. The slight glimmer of stars or satellites or planets or something else entirely breaking up the devouring depths of space. The Earth below us, Australia and some of the islands of the south Pacific clearly visible, New Zealand peeking up from the side.

I moaned, but the sound was softer.

'Breathe, Tessa. That's it,' Cy whispered.

I held the image in my mind, letting myself grow used to it. It was just a different way of seeing, I told myself. I was just up higher than I'd been before. And though space looked empty, I knew it wasn't. The moon was waiting somewhere, and past that, Mars and the rest of the planets in the solar system. And beyond that –

I choked back a sob and pressed my face into Cy's shirt.

At some stage, I realised that his words had changed. He wasn't just murmuring my name; he was telling me how brave I was, how beautiful, how strong and warm and captivating. He told me how much he wanted me – how much *they* wanted me – and how it had felt when he'd walked into my apartment and saw my face for the first time. He told me how he loved my smile, and the colour of my eyes, and how my hair curled around my face.

'You can't just say things like that, Cy,' I croaked.

His arms tightened. 'Tell me what you need, Tessa.'

I was silent for a moment. 'Is it always like that?' I said eventually. 'So ... big?'

'It's always like that,' he murmured. 'I shut off my fear response the first time I saw it. Aster and Morgan are used to big things. The heavens are Aster's playground, and Morgan can swim so far down that the water turns black and the sharks are bigger than buildings. But all I'd known was Machina – my cubicle and my classroom and my allocated park and the number of steps between each. I'd never ever seen the sea – I lived too far into the city, and sightseeing wasn't in our vocabulary. I was so scared when Aster jumped me up into the ship, Tessa. All I could think of was the black. That, and *what if I've made a mistake*?'

'How did you know you hadn't?' I choked out.

'Aster knew I couldn't keep my fear response deactivated long-term; it has flow-on hormonal effects that damage both my organic and computer systems. So he waited. And when I turned it back on, and everything hit me – all the feelings I'd repressed – he made a nest in the bedroom and held me for two days while I cried. Beings aren't *always* brave or *always* scared, Tessa. Most beings move between the two every day of their lives. I learned to deal with the black over time. It was some months before I was comfortable looking out, and even longer before I could pilot. But Aster and Morgan were by my side every time I needed them.'

I shuddered. 'I don't think ... I don't think I can, Cy.'

He took a deep breath. 'I understand.' He held me tightly. 'I understand.'

My heart broke.

I reached up and kissed him, because I didn't want to think. He nuzzled at my lips with a tenderness that made my chest ache, responding to every movement I made so perfectly that I felt like I was floating in his arms.

I realised then that though all three of them *wanted* an *elyn*, wanted *balance*, it was Cy who really *needed* it. Morgan and Aster were loud, brave, brash, confident. They took the world in their stride; from what I'd learned, they'd been bought up to do it. With two of them and only one of Cy, his sweetness, his gentleness, his shyness, and his *quiet* were overpowered. They were like a three-legged stool, and Cy was wobbling, always questioning what he felt; he needed another leg to stabilise him, to let him know that his gentleness was as important as the others' bravery.

Can I be that? I wondered. *Can I help him stay strong? Can I help him discover himself?*

'I've been thinking,' he whispered against my lips.

'What have you been thinking?'

'You've been asking what it will be like if you come with us, but I think there's another question you should consider.'

'What question?'

He kissed me again, the softest brush of his lips over my cheek. 'What will it be like if you stay?'

ASTER

Cy TREMBLED AS I put my arm around him. Morgan was more stoic, still as calm water, but I could feel how he'd tensed up, how tight his muscles were. Tessa was crying again, but silently, like she was trying to smother what she was feeling.

My heart hurt. It seemed unfair that something I'd *created* could cause me so much pain.

'I'll take them up, then bring you back the screen,' I promised her. She wasn't coming with us, but Cy had several spare screens that she could keep and use to send us messages.

If she wanted to.

She nodded, her bottom lip between her teeth, her eyes bright with tears.

'Goodbye, *elyn*,' Cy whispered. Morgan said nothing, just brushed his fingers over her cheek one final time.

I knew it would be worse if we drew it out, so I let my trueform bleed through my humanoid costume. Tessa inhaled sharply as the lines of me began to pulse with darklight. I let the starlight in me call to the starlight – the star*dust* – inside Morgan and Cy, let it come to the fore and dissolve them.

There was a saying common across the universe: *we are the stars*. I knew that Earth had its own version of the saying, and it was entirely true. But I was *literally* born in a dying star, my form made of its decaying light and given life anew, and that meant that I could call to the stars within other beings, too. My loves exploded into light around me, and I swept them up – and *up* – until their stars and mine were safely nestled in our ship's bedroom, then I loosened my hold and let their light revert back to their trueforms.

Cy staggered, and I held him firm. Morgan tore himself from my grip and collapsed to sit on the bed, his head in his hands.

'It's not right,' Cy said thickly. 'How could this happen? We're *made* for her, and her for us.'

'I know, handsome,' I murmured, and stroked his cropped hair. The stars were loud again, singing an angry, mournful dirge at the separation, every note tinged with *wrongness*.

Morgan rubbed his face roughly. 'We will be grateful for the time we had,' he said. 'Better to have tried and failed than to have never known her at all.'

I pressed a hand over my heart. 'We'll come back,' I vowed. 'Five years isn't so long.'

'For us.' Cy folded to sit next to Morgan, taking the prince in his arms. 'Five years is longer for her. You heard what she said. She could find a mate and bear them children in that time.'

'It won't matter,' I said loyally. 'An *elyn* doesn't have to be that kind of partner. An *elyn* can be –'

'We know what an *elyn* can be, Aster,' Morgan growled. 'Just as much as *you* know that doesn't apply to us.' He kissed Cy's head. 'I want her so badly it hurts. Every part of her. In every way.'

I pressed on my heart again. 'We shouldn't wait too long to take the screen back,' I said, changing the subject, because I knew Morgan was right. Could I bear to see Tessa mated to another human? Heat flared under my skin as I considered it, scalding and angry, and I supposed not. I shook my head to clear it. 'Cy? The screen?'

Cy gave an audible swallow. 'I'll find one,' he said, and got up, walking from the room as if he'd suddenly aged a thousand years.

Morgan pulled me into his lap, hissing briefly at how hot my skin was. 'We failed,' he said hoarsely, as I pressed my forehead to his. 'We failed. And our failure hurt Cy.'

I kissed his closed eyes. 'We'll make it better,' I vowed. 'We'll make everything better for him. Every single day, that's what we'll work for. To make Cy happy. We'll take him back to the summer nest and let him hack into the Darnargh databases like he was talking about last month. He said their protections were the best in the universe.'

Morgan's lips tugged up in the smallest smile I'd ever seen. 'That will keep him busy for about a week.'

'Then we'll find him another system,' I said wildly. 'We'll get him whatever he needs to build a better one. I'll do anything, Mor. This is all my fault.'

'Aster, you tide-addled prawn,' Morgan said fondly. 'Of course it isn't.' He put his hand over my heart and kissed me gently. 'This will be a wound. With time it will scar. It won't ever leave, but we can learn to live with it. The sky will seem brighter just knowing she exists. That will have to be enough.'

I kissed him back fiercely, trying not to sob. It *wasn't* enough, not for me, and I knew it wasn't for him. It would *never* be enough.

'Got it,' Cy said softly.

I gave Morgan one more rough kiss and disentangled myself, taking the small screen from Cy.

'This one looks more like a smartphone,' he said, his voice low and even; I wondered if he'd turned his emotion receptors off. 'I thought it would be unlikely to generate suspicion from other humans. I've made it so she'll be able to contact the ship's communication system, and our own personal screens. We'll be able to pick up the signal on Natare, though I'll have to re-route it through their satellites once we get back and scramble the trail so no one will pick it up and follow it back to her.' He bit his lip. 'I also set up a bank account she can access. I hate ...' He trailed off and took a deep breath. 'I hate the thought of her wanting. She can quit her job if she chooses, and go back to university like she was talking about.'

I cupped his cheek. 'That's a good idea, handsome,' I said softly. I had a suspicion that Tessa wouldn't touch the money, but it was a nice thought, nevertheless. I took the screen from him, turning it over in my hand; I closed my eyes for a moment. 'I should get this over with so we can leave before the Tirians arrive.' I surveyed them both; Cy, looking more mechanic than usual as he stood with blank eyes and a stiff pose, and Morgan, unapologetically bowed with grief on the bed. 'I love you both.'

I dissolved into my trueform before they could reply, reforming moments later in Tessa's sitting room.

It was empty; I frowned.

'Tessa?' I called warily. 'It's Aster; I have the screen for you.'

There was no answer.

I closed my eyes. I could see her heat through the wall. I dissolved again and jumped the handful of metres, reforming behind her as she stared into her bathroom mirror.

Her face was blank. 'It's wrong,' she said flatly.

'What's wrong, *elyn*?'

'This,' she said, gesturing at the mirror. 'Me.'

'Nothing about you is *wrong*,' I growled, sounding rather too much like Morgan for my liking.

'When I saw us all together, it looked *right*,' she went on, ignoring me. 'It looked like something that should be. It looked like something I *wanted*. But this,' she said, gesturing to her reflection again, 'me, *alone*, it's *wrong*. It looks all wrong, Aster.'

I froze as hope rose like a wave inside me.

'You've changed everything,' she snapped crossly at my reflection, her eyes flickering between furious and resolved. 'In one single night, you've changed *everything*. I can't go back from that, star-man. How am I supposed to function, knowing you're all out there somewhere, *together*, and I'm not with you? How could I function, knowing you exist but I can't touch you? How could I live when you've changed my entire world? When you've gone, but you're still in my heart?'

The stars sang their triumph, deafening.

Tessa turned to me. 'How fast can you help me pack?'

She left two messages. One was handwritten on a piece of silver paper; the other, a text.

Dear Maeve,
There's no easy way to say this – I'm going trav-
elling. I'm safe, I'm happy, and I've chosen this.
I've left you my car (sorry ...) and my debit card,
with enough money to cover rent for the next
three months (and then some). It's all yours. I'll
keep in touch when I can.
Thank you for everything you've done for me.
Love, Tessa.
P.S. I found some new dresses. Three of them, to
be exact. I'm going to see how long I can wear
them.

Hey Rian, just want to let you know that I'm
going on a trip overseas. I don't know when I'll
be able to text again, but I'll try to email. Let me
know how your first week as a detective goes! <3

We'd packed everything we could: clothes, books, memen-
tos, and enough hair care products to sink an airship. I'd tried
to convince her to leave her hair straightener behind – I had
the feeling Morgan would try to throw it into the nearest
patch of darkspace as soon as he got his hands on it, and
I wasn't entirely sure we could plug it in – but other than
that, I'd been mostly helpful as we'd folded her clothes and
packed her books into boxes and cleaned her room and the
apartment, so everything was tidy for her housemate.

'Are you ready?' I said, once her bedroom was looking
rather more sparse than before.

Tessa pulled on a pair of boots with stiletto heels that could take an eye out. They were her favourite, apparently; I liked how they made her slightly taller, and therefore easier to kiss. 'Can you be ready and not-ready at the same time?'

I took advantage of her extra height and brushed my lips over her hair. 'You can be anything you want to be, *elyn*.'

Her screen was going wild with messages from Cy, demanding to know where I was, and what was taking so long. I was already sorry that I'd caused him and Morgan extra worry, but I was about to bring them the best surprise in the entire universe, so my regret wasn't that long-lived.

'Aster,' she said hesitantly, chewing her bottom lip.

I stroked her cheek. 'Mmm?'

'How long do you think it takes to fall in love?'

'For you? I don't know.' I brushed my lips over hers. 'For me? I fall as soon as the stars sing, Tessa. They've never steered me wrong.'

She searched my face. 'Are they singing now?'

I smiled. 'They've been singing non-stop all night. They think we're exactly where we need to be.'

She wrapped her arms around my neck. 'I'm ready.'

I kissed her hair one final time, and let my starlight bleed over my *elyn* and everything she'd packed, and I took us up.

I stilled over the city, taking in the sprawling lights and the incessant humanity that filled the structures. Studying the skyline, something caught my eye. Something coloured silver – something that shouldn't be there.

The Tirians had arrived early.

Their huge, ringed ship with its glass dome lurked over the Australian eastern coastline. Their simple presence was threat enough.

Time to go, I thought.

I took us up, and *up*, before I let my hold loosen and her light revert back to her trueform on our bed.

Tessa squeaked in surprise, finding herself in a nest of Morgan's limbs. I laughed myself stupid as he swore in shock, then realised who it was and swore again, wrapping his limbs tight around her and pulling her against his chest.

I disappeared to get a bucket, letting them have their moment before I reappeared and thrust the bucket under Tessa's mouth just as she began to retch. Morgan held her through it, his limbs like thick ropes around her body, as Cy appeared in the doorway to see what the noise was.

And crumpled to his knees.

I rushed to his side and wrapped my arms around him as he shook. He held onto me like I was an anchor, a lifeline. 'Aster –'

'Shh,' I soothed. 'Your *elyn* changed her mind. She's here. But the Tirians are, too; we need to leave.'

He looked up at me. 'You don't think –'

'No, handsome,' I said. I pressed my forehead to his. 'They'll never get their hands on you, Cy. I promise.'

He swallowed. 'Machina has increased the reward for my capture. I checked before we left the ship.'

I scoffed. 'You're worth *far* more than the price they've promised. I don't think the Tirians are here for you. I think our ship appeared on their radar, and they're making sure we're not breaking any rules.'

'We are, though,' he pointed out. 'Tessa shouldn't be on board. We are very definitely breaking multiple laws.'

'You can alter the ship's records, can't you?'

He thought for a moment. 'Darnargh,' he said. 'I can alter the records and list her as Darnargh.'

'My clever love,' I murmured. The Darnargh were humanoid, and close enough to humans that long-range scanners wouldn't be able to tell the difference. It would only be a problem if we were pulled up for a spot check, as Tessa very obviously lacked the tail the Darnargh boasted, but as spot checks came with a hefty amount of bureaucratic processing – read: paperwork – the Tirians would only board us if we did something obviously wrong.

Like staying in Earth's orbit for too long.

Cy had turned back to Tessa, and was scanning her form as she finished retching. 'Water,' he croaked. 'Water and a wafer.'

'I'll get them.' I pulled him to his feet. 'Go to her.'

I didn't wait to see if he did, walking to the kitchen to fill a glass and take a mouth wafer from the dispenser rather than dissolving so I could give the three of them a moment together. I was glad I had; Cy had evidently turned his receptors back on and was on his knees at the side of the bed, his face pressed to Tessa's stomach as she stroked his hair. I held the glass so that she could drink, then slipped the wafer between her lips when she opened her mouth. I disappeared for a moment into the space outside the ship, taking the bucket with me to empty it, reforming it as new in the storage room once I was done.

Tessa's expression was flickering rapidly as I went back to the bedroom, shifting between happiness and shock.

'It's done, isn't it?' she whispered. 'I've left. I've left forever.'

'Not forever, not if you don't want to,' Cy answered, his voice muffled against her stomach. 'You can come back in five years. Or Aster could bring you back sooner if you needed.'

She swallowed. 'Five years,' she repeated. 'I can do five years.' She sniffed, then squared her shoulders, gently disentangling herself from Morgan's limbs. 'I want to see the cockpit again.'

'You don't have to do that –' I started.

She got up off the bed, and walked straight out the door, pausing only to pick up Cy's pillow from the bed to take with her, hugging it to her chest.

'Fuck,' I said, and we scrambled to follow her.

Morgan had evidently started the flight sequence while I'd been helping Tessa pack; the control panel lights flashed as Cy synced to their systems and prompted our engine to start rumbling gently in readiness. Tessa glanced at the lights, then stepped down into the cockpit.

She faltered when she fixed on the stretch of glass and the black beyond it, whimpering softly.

'Starfish,' Morgan growled, then reached out and took her hand. He shifted back into his humanoid form, sliding onto the pilot's bench and pulling Tessa down with him, arranging her legs so that she straddled his hips.

'Pillow, Tessa,' he said.

She handed Cy the pillow. 'I want that back,' she warned.

Morgan took her chin and raised it. 'Tell me why you're afraid,' he commanded. 'I can smell it.'

'It's too big,' she said.

'What is?'

'Everything.'

He studied her for a moment. 'Yes,' he said. 'It's big. It goes forever. There are more worlds than you can count, more species than you can imagine. Your planet is there, below you.' His hand shifted, cupping her cheek. 'But we are here.'

She exhaled.

'We are here,' he repeated. 'You can hear our hearts, feel our skin, see our light. We are here for *you*. *Just* for you, Tessa. Anything you need.' He kissed her brow, then her nose, then her lips. Then, without warning, he lifted her knees and spun her, pressing her back against his chest. His hand settled over her eyes before she saw anything; his free arm wrapped around her waist. 'The black might be big,' he whispered, 'but we conquered it to find *you*.'

'You fucking sweetheart,' I muttered, my chest feeling rather tight.

Cy took one of her hands; I hastened to grab the other. 'We have you, *elyn*,' Cy said softly.

Morgan took his hand away from her eyes. She kept them closed for a heartbeat longer, then opened them a crack and peered through her lashes.

She took in the black, then the Earth. A stretch of cloud obscured New Zealand.

Morgan settled his chin on her shoulder. 'It's beautiful, no?'

'Yes,' she breathed.

He swept her hair from her neck and settled his mouth on her pulse. 'Not half as beautiful as you.'

She snorted. 'Liar.'

He bit her gently. 'Do you want to go back?'

'No,' she said immediately.

Morgan nodded. 'Forwards it is, then.'

I looked out and saw the four of us reflected in the glass. My eyes met Tessa's, and I realised that she wasn't looking down at the Earth at all; she wasn't looking at the black, endless stretch of space, or at the stars. She was looking at us, at the reflection of the four of us together, our forms lit by the dim lights of the control panel. She gave me the tiniest smile, as if we were sharing a secret.

I slid into the seat next to Morgan, grinning. 'In the Earth screencasts, the aliens always probe the humans. Do I get to probe you now?'

Tessa smacked my knee, then appeared to think about it. 'Maybe later.'

TESSA

I ROLLED OVER AND groaned softly.

Beside me, Cy adjusted soundlessly, moving his body so that I had enough space but he was still touching me, his hand warm and heavy on my waist. I threw my arm out, searching for Morgan, but the bed was cold.

I opened my eyes.

Aster was above us, floating in a vaguely man-shaped mass of the darkest black. The first night on the ship he'd taken me up with him, and I'd woken, floating four feet off the bed wrapped in darkness, and screamed myself hoarse until he'd flared awake and dropped me unceremoniously back on the mattress in shock. It had happened a few times since then, and I'd learned to deal with it. For a being made of light, Aster made a surprisingly comfortable pillow, and I liked the way he wove himself around me.

I sat up and rubbed my eyes.

'Don't go yet,' Cy mumbled immediately. Technically, Cy didn't need to sleep, but he had a setting that mimicked the state while his systems ran checks. He was apparently as susceptible to viruses as any Earth computer, but he had assured me that his firewall equivalents were *much* more sophisticated.

'Is Morgan in the pit?' I whispered.

'He should be.'

'Then I'm going for a swim. I need to wash my hair.'

Aster dropped down onto the bed, shifting to his human form mid-air, and curled himself around Cy. Cy murmured wordlessly and pulled the starling's arms tight around him.

I smiled at them, my heart swelling. They were so beautiful together. All that was missing was my grumpy blonde cephalopod.

But if he was busy checking the flight systems, then I might finally be allowed to wash my hair by myself.

I had quickly learned that the pool really *was* Morgan's domain, and he ruled it like a merciless king. His caring manifested in a number of ways – he would make me glasses of water, cups of tea, or a plate full of nutrient snacks even before I even knew I wanted them – but in the pool his caring manifested more *intimately*. Not just as hair-washing, but as massages, and – once he discovered my nail polish collection and demanded to know what the small bottles were for – as manicures and pedicures.

Most of the time, I lay back in the water and enjoyed being so spoiled; it was like being at the best salon in the world, where your wash ended with a back rub and an orgasm. This time, though, there were a handful of other things I wanted to do – tinting my brows and lashes, waxing my bikini line – and I wanted to do them myself. I drew the line at Morgan *waxing* me.

The other thing I wanted was simpler – just half an hour properly alone. On a ship with five small rooms and four people taking them up, alone time could be hard to find. The pool was the only room that you could fully seal and let yourself relax. Everyone needed time to be alone, no matter how much they adored the people around them.

Cy put up with Morgan's caring good-naturedly, but I'd realised that he was quite strict about stealing time in the pool while the Enterocti prince was piloting or running system checks in the cockpit. Sometimes I wondered if Cy wasn't causing slight problems in the systems just to make sure his alone time happened; the ship seemed to run beautifully for the most part. Aster had negotiated a once-a-month, three-hour window where Morgan was allowed to subject him to a personal spa day, and told him blatantly to fuck off if Morgan went so much as half a minute past it.

I'd watched them closely over the last six weeks. They both had different ways they handled Morgan's instincts. Aster chose to fight him until Morgan's hunter came to the fore and their battle dissolved into underwear-melting bouts of sex; Cy worked around them, submitting to them just enough to satisfy Morgan, but not so much that Cy lost sense of himself and his own wants.

I was still working it out. And Morgan was, if anything, the most straightforward of the three. It was just like any normal relationship, where you learned to live with and around the other person's strengths and quirks, but in this case, I was learning to live with *three* other people, and them with me.

Surprisingly, the species differences didn't often come into it; I'd certainly met humans who were much, *much* stranger.

I found a towel and pressed my hand to the bedroom wall. The door slid open, then closed once more when I stepped through. I could smell peppermint tea coming from the kitchen; Morgan wouldn't touch my coffee, but he'd developed a taste for Earth herbal teas. Cy had kept all the tiny packets so he could program the generators to replicate them once we arrived at Natare.

It had taken a few weeks for the thrill of being on the ship to fade. I had spent days sitting in the pit – either with someone, or alone when they were doing something else – simply watching the black expanse of space as we flew distances I couldn't begin to comprehend. Cy showed me how to work the viewing system, and I spent hours focusing on specific parts of space around us, zooming in on planets and galaxies and moons and – one memorable day turned existential crisis – on a black hole.

You don't want to do that, starlight, Aster had said, taking the viewing control gently away from me. *Even my kind don't do that. Black holes aren't for mortals. We leave them be.*

I'd brought my tablet, and Cy had downloaded – well, the entire *internet* onto the ship's server. *Just in case you need it,* he said. When I'd protested that I didn't need *all* of it, and that there was, in fact, quite a lot of it I would be glad to never see again, he'd smiled sadly. *You never know what you'll want in the future.*

I couldn't stand to see Cy sad, so I'd spent some weeks watching content he'd downloaded so he knew I'd appreciated his efforts. When I started to get bored of that, he began researching the equivalent of universities for me. They didn't work the way I was familiar with; they were all delivered something like online, for one, only with way better options than the pre-recorded lectures I was used to. I'd thought that I wanted to stick with art history – or an alien version of it – but when I thought about it more, I realised that I now had an entire *universe* of knowledge that I could access. I hadn't made a decision, because I had too much choice. Did I apply for cross-galaxy philosophy? Comparative physics? Non-organic biology? Deep-space archaeology? Poetry of the stars? Beginner's robotics?

Cy had wrinkled his nose at the last one. *I can teach you that.*

Imagine the practicals, Aster had said, winking.

I shivered.

Practicals with Cy were still a work in progress, requiring single-minded determination and a whole lot of lube. He'd learned my body astonishingly quickly, and seemed to take a kind of smug pleasure in the fact he could make me moan with his fingers in under a minute – Aster had timed it. Cy would blush a beautiful pink as he worked his cock inside me afterwards, stopping halfway, just before it became too much, then moving in shallow, gentle thrusts until he made me moan again.

Aster spent most of his time cataloguing the sounds I made and tormenting me with imitations of them at random times during the day, but I got my revenge by doing a fair approximation of the face he'd made the first time I'd gone down on him, which seemed to be the only thing that would make *him* blush. I had always disliked giving head before, as I'd felt all the power imbalance of it, and I *hated* when someone took my hair in their hands and tried to guide me, but Aster only had to throw a side-eyed, glowing glance my way to have my mouth watering and my eyes wandering towards his crotch. I did it as often as I could; he'd shift his size so I could take him in my mouth comfortably, something I couldn't do with the other two. He always reciprocated, and seemed to delight in spreading me out in the cockpit while Morgan was piloting in an attempt to distract the cephalopod.

Morgan was, without fail, happy to be distracted. I'd worked out very swiftly that he wore his heart on his sleeve, and he threw himself headfirst into everything he did. Which meant, in this instance, us. He was persistent and single-minded and dogged, and he worked until he wrung us dry.

I had no complaints. I also had the feeling that Maeve would approve. Of all three of my males, and of everything else.

I used the bathroom – the toilet-looking thing *was* a toilet, Cy had confirmed, though I would have found out for myself; Morgan – perhaps entirely unsurprisingly – did not often shut the door. Aster found the subject of bodily waste hilarious, and smugly disappeared outside the ship whenever he felt the need to *reset his form*. I didn't really want to know what that entailed, only that it seemed to cover both eating and everything else all at once; I didn't see how that was any *less* gross.

A loud moan issued from the bedroom as I walked into the pool room. It was Aster, and it was the groan he gave whenever one of us wrapped a hand around his cock. I paused, imagining Cy's fingers around Aster's length. One hand went up, rubbing over a nipple.

'Hair now,' I muttered to myself. 'Sex later.'

The lights in the pool room were dimmed. The water rippled calmly, the near-silent sigh of the overflow echoing gently off the walls.

'Morgan?' I whispered.

There was no answer. The water was unbroken; there were no bubbles anywhere. I narrowed my eyes.

'Morgan, if you're in there ...' I started warningly.

There was no response.

I studied the shapes of the rocks beneath the surface, and watched the barely-perceptible sway of the kelp. It all looked normal, but I knew that Morgan could hold his breath for an indecently long time in either of his forms, and camouflage his limbs to match his surroundings.

'I swear to God, Morgan.'

Morgan liked to care; he also liked to *hunt*. I knew the rules: if so much as a toe touched the water and he was in there, I was fair game.

The water didn't change.

I set down my towel and stripped off, pulling Cy's shirt over my head. Between the three of them, they'd almost succeeded in Morgan's quest to see me go without underwear; more pairs than I could count had been ripped in two. I'd like to think it was all in haste, but I was fairly sure they'd planned it. It meant I slept without, which no one complained about, including me. There was something magical about rubbing up against a hard cock while you were still half asleep and having to do nothing more than murmur *yes, please* and part your knees to feel it inside you.

'Morgan,' I said sternly one more time, but received no reply. I inched towards the water.

The very tip of my big toe touched the drain.

The surface erupted.

I shrieked as a limb knocked me off my feet. I was immediately caught by a second, and cushioned by a third, then dragged through the cool water until I was wrapped up in thick sea-green flesh.

'Morning, starfish,' Morgan whispered in my ear.

I struggled. *'Morgan,'* I whined, panting.

'You know the rules, Tessa,' he rumbled. 'Are you in or out?'

They were all aware of human consent, and took enforcing it *very* seriously. Aster's kind communicated via light waves in their trueforms, and *the exchange of light* – their equivalent of sex, however the fuck it worked – took place only in long-term relationships based on total trust and transparency. Cyborgs donated their genetic material to special baby-making factories – I'd not slept for a week after I'd watched the screencasts of how they melded the tiny organic bodies with the mechanic and computer systems – and didn't usually have sex, despite having been originally built for just that purpose.

Morgan's species was different again, mating only during a heat, for weeks at a time, driven by instinct and scent, not attraction and consent. When Morgan learned how different human practices were, he'd taken asking for permission so seriously that he checked with me every time he kissed my cheek or moved his hand on my hip. I didn't mind – the fact he went against his own nature to make sure I felt safe and respected made my heart swell – but it made everything *very* slow. And sometimes I just wanted him inside me. Immediately. Hard.

We'd talked it through and found a middle ground. He asked me *in or out?* before anything started, and I reserved the right to change my mind at any time. He could smell how I was feeling, anyway, and he pulled back immediately if he sensed I wasn't fully into it. Getting my period had blown his mind; his expression when he'd scented me – in pain and angry and sad and horny all at once – had been one of the funniest things I'd ever seen. He didn't understand how I could want him when I was bleeding. Cy had taken over and touched me gently, murmuring to Morgan about human hormones and cramps and how orgasms could sometimes help relax the muscles and relieve the pain. Morgan had been on board after that. Aster bled light, not blood, and had watched, fascinated, as Cy and then Morgan had gotten me off, and then Cy had disappeared to make me a cup of tea and get some of my precious chocolate.

Morgan wasn't the only one who spoiled me.

'Starfish,' Morgan growled.

I sighed and reached up to bunch his hair in my hand. 'In, Morgan.' I tugged on his blonde locks. 'But will you paint my toenails, please?'

He rumbled a pleased growl. 'Do I get to choose the colour?'

'No.'

He bit me gently on the neck. It was a bonding thing for his kind, the scar a physical symbol of their lifelong commitment. When their fangs broke the skin, they'd seal the wound with their venom, which would both heal the wound in a raised scar and stop the need to respond to other mating heats. They'd respond to their mate – or, in Morgan's case, mates – and no other. I turned in his arms and bit him back, gently at first, then so hard he gasped. His limbs tightened around me.

'You're asking for trouble, Tessa,' he growled.

'You did it first,' I answered, licking up the column of his throat.

He tilted his head back and let me bite a trail up his jugular. He liked being in charge, but he liked it even more when I played at being dominant. I liked it, too.

There was supposed to be a ceremony involved to formalise the biting-come-bonding, with candles and offerings to Natare's watery gods. It was supposed to happen as soon as the pair came out of their mating heat, and it sounded pretty similar to a wedding, really. But I'd watched Morgan bite the back of Cy's neck the last time they'd fucked, and it had veered excitingly close to the real thing; Cy's silvery blood had been visible under the bruises. I wonder what it would take for Morgan to crack and bite for real.

Do we get to bite you back? I'd asked.

We didn't, apparently, but what we *did* get to do was choose where a tattoo would mimic our bite marks on his body. Morgan had hopefully suggested that all three went on his neck, so all of Natare would know their prince was taken; Aster had countered that Morgan probably shouldn't remind his people that his mates comprised of Machina's most wanted hacker and an abductee from a planet that wasn't supposed to know there was life outside its galaxy. Morgan wasn't entirely convinced; his last suggestion had been around his wrist, which – given the nature of his uniform, as Cy had described it to me – was just as conspicuous.

I bit Morgan again, right above the collarbone. He groaned and grabbed my ass, pulling me tight against him. I ground my clit against his rock-hard stomach and rubbed myself over the limb making itself at home between my legs.

It slipped away, swiftly replaced by one that was just a little thicker, and just a little longer. I surged up to capture his lips immediately. He didn't always use his mating shaft; like the massive softie he was, he saved it for when we were *making love* rather than fucking.

He kissed me deeply, thoroughly, and with a reverent slowness that brought tears to my eyes, wrapping his arms so tight around me that I began panting. He trailed kisses over my jaw and up the shell of my ear, his mating shaft rubbing slowly over my entrance and up to my clit, the tip of it pressing down.

'Morgan, babe, now, do it now,' I moaned.

The tip played outside my opening, driving me wild. If we'd been outside the water, I would have drenched it with my readiness. As it was, his mating shaft produced its own lubricant, which was convenient for both of us. 'Do what, Tessa?' he rumbled. He dipped the tip inside me; my breath hitched. 'That?'

'More,' I begged. 'Morgan, *more*.'

He gave me what I wanted; he always did. Aster would tease me for hours, making me sweat and whimper and beg, and even Cy sometimes enjoyed making me work for it, but Morgan always gave me exactly what I wanted, exactly when I wanted it.

His shaft pushed slowly inside, his suckers pressing rhythmically against every sweet spot, thrusting gently until I was stretched wide around it. Even after weeks of almost non-stop sex, there was still a slight burn, but it was sweet. Morgan knew, and the tip of another limb came up to trail over my stretched skin, back and forth, until the burn became a delicious tingle as the tip inside me curled, filling me completely. I whined and wriggled my hips until he groaned.

'You're dangerous, starfish,' he growled. He thrust until I threw my head back and whimpered.

His hands fell to my hips, encouraging me to move, to take what I wanted from him. I rolled my hips, locking my knees around his waist and my arms around his neck, using him as leverage to move my body.

'Fuck, Tessa, *yes*,' he hissed. I knew he loved it deep and slow, so I kept my movements rolling and fluid, both my hands reaching up to fist handfuls of his blonde hair.

Another limb slid up my thigh and cupped my ass, its suckers fluttering against my skin. It toyed with my flesh and gave me a playful slap, before sliding towards my core.

My breath caught as its tip traced over my sensitive skin. The feeling drove me wild; my hips bucked.

'Yes or no, beautiful?'

'Yes,' I gasped. 'Morgan. Yes.'

The tip pushed inside me, gently stretching past the tight ring of muscle. I didn't want it all the time, but saying that ass play was a group strength was an understatement.

'That's it,' he murmured. He didn't move any further, just held me as I rocked back and forth, fucking his limbs further inside myself.

Sweat broke out on my forehead as my body began to feel divinely, almost unbearably full. He began to move slowly and carefully, pushing one limb in further as he slid the other back. His suckers moved continually in a series of soft flutters. 'Morgan,' I moaned, 'please.'

'Please what, gorgeous?'

I'd meant to say *make me come*, but what came out was: 'Bite me. Do it now.'

He shuddered; his fingers embedded themselves in the flesh of my hips. *'Tessa,'* he groaned. 'You can't just say that. We need to do it together.' He kissed my collarbone. 'Fuck, I want it so badly.'

'Do it,' I begged. 'Morgan. Do it.'

He shook his head. 'No, starfish,' he whispered. 'I hate saying no to you. But I want it to be all of us.'

'Cy and Aster are probably fucking right now,' I said, and ground my hips, making myself cry out as bliss radiated through my core. 'Get them in here.'

He took my chin. 'I want us to be together, Tessa,' he repeated, laying emphasis on the word. 'Like we are right now. Are you ready for that?'

I went still for a moment, then rolled my hips again. *Together*. Like, all at once. A foursome type together, which we hadn't attempted yet. Which would presumably mean me in the middle, impaled on two cocks, or a cock and a tentacle.

I rolled my hips forward and ground my clit against him, coming with a sobbing cry.

'*Fuck*,' he swore, caught off guard as I pushed him over, my body pulsing around his mating shaft; a moment later, cool bliss spread inside me as he pumped me full of jellied cum. His mating shaft was the only limb he came from, but it produced twice to three times more than its human equivalent, doing its best to ensure the continuance of his species. A large quantity flooded out of me as he shifted slightly; I lay my head on his shoulder.

'I guess you don't hate that idea, then,' he said dryly.

'I do not hate that idea.' I rubbed my cheek on his skin. 'How would it work?'

'Cy is too big for you at the moment,' he said immediately, letting me know exactly how much thought he'd given this. 'Aster can change his size, which might make it more comfortable for you here.' He gently withdrew from my back passage; I squirmed. 'So I'll be here –' he reached down and stroked my clit and flesh stretching deliciously around him, making no attempt to move his shaft '– and Cy can fuck who he likes. But I hope it's me. It's my mating day, after all. Aster can have a turn the next time.'

'Such a good sharer,' I cooed.

He poked me in the ribs, which made me giggle and squirm. He groaned as my internal muscles flexed and pulled at his shaft. 'I did that to myself,' he muttered, and pulled out of me, using another limb to wrap around my waist and shift me sideways on his lap. Another came up to pour water over my hair, its tip curled around to create a cup.

I sighed and tipped my head back so he could start washing. 'You're going to choose the nail polish colour, aren't you?'

He laughed. 'Tessa, starfish, I'd chosen it before you even walked in.'

MORGAN

TESSA PULLED HERSELF FROM the pool with shaking arms some hours later. I didn't try to help her, even though my instincts screamed at me to assist my mate; she'd explained to me a few weeks ago that although she understood that I was being protective – that I was *cherishing* her – it made her feel infantilised instead, and she was perfectly capable of getting out of the pool by herself. Her hair was shining from the stuff I'd worked through it – a *masque*, Tessa called it – and she was freshly divested of upper leg hair, though I was still working out why she found *that* necessary. Her fingers and toes were painted with a pearly apricot-pink – almost like the inside of an oyster shell – which she admitted she liked better than the bright red she'd suggested.

I liked seeing her in the colours of the ocean. There *were* types of red coral, but most of them were poisonous, and I couldn't stop shuddering whenever I saw that bright shade, my survival instincts screaming *do not touch*. Which, when it came to Tessa, was the *opposite* of how I actually felt. It was a constant struggle to keep my hands and limbs off her, a struggle I only sometimes won.

'Fuck, Morgan, I can barely walk,' she muttered, staggering to her feet without her usual composed grace.

'Mmm,' I rumbled in agreement, smiling lazily.

She glared at me as she pulled on a shirt. 'I'm going to find Cy,' she said with an arch sniff.

'To tell him that I beat his record?'

'Humans aren't made for *seven* orgasms, Morgan. *Three* is more than sufficient.' She paused. 'And I really wish Aster would stop keeping count.'

'I disagree,' I yawned, showing my fangs. 'About all those things.'

She hissed as arousal bloomed again between her legs. 'Urgh. How could I possibly want you again?' She looked down. 'You have a death wish, I swear it,' she said to herself. 'I *will* need a vagina transplant if you keep this up.'

'You could always go and find Aster,' I said, smirking. 'He'll make it better.'

Tessa had gone through her supply of condoms fairly swiftly – the boxes were empty by the third night – and although Cy had offered to make a replacement, she'd decided to stop using them. Cy had dissolved her contraceptive implant, and had used a healing wand to build tiny barriers of organic material to block her fallopian tubes instead. Tessa loved it; it had no hormonal or physical side-effects, none of the cramps or headaches or mood swings she'd grown used to.

Which all meant that we could come inside her with im- punity. Cy had already tested all of us for any disease we could pass on, and was running surreptitious tests to see whether our genetics were similar enough for children. I didn't know how Tessa felt about it yet; I didn't want to raise the possibility if it was never going to happen. Cy had indicated that the results so far had been positive, but cautioned that he wasn't done with all the projections yet and that he wanted *a real doctor to check them*, so I shouldn't get too excited.

But Cy had noticed something else, too. After Tessa had spent a night with Aster on the floor of the cockpit – not sleeping – he'd frowned in surprise.

Elyn, your operation scars are gone, he'd blurted. He'd studied her with the fixed gaze I knew as him running scans of her body. *And the break in your toe. And your endometriosis.*

And so he'd watched for a while, in typical Cy fashion, stashing away every detail in his massive, complex brain. Fucking *me* had no effect on Tessa that wasn't expected, and fucking Cy made her happy but sore; fucking Aster, however, had an entirely different result.

He *healed* her.

Well, not him. His cum. Because Aster was born in a star, all his body matter was made of starlight and stardust, and apparently its introduction into the human body had Tessa's immune systems *resetting* itself so thoroughly that every and all imperfections were entirely fixed.

I'm going to fuck you until you're immortal, Aster had said to Tessa, when Cy had put forward his theory.

Cy wasn't sure it would work that way, although he didn't discount it, either. If Aster could *keep* Tessa's systems resetting, she might theoretically live far longer than humans were supposed to.

Which gave the three of us silent hope in the face of a worry we hadn't yet voiced. Cy would live until his system wore out, which could be hundreds of thousands of years. Starlings seemed to end their own existences in around the same time frame, growing tired of living once nothing seemed new anymore. My own kind were fairly long-lived; my grandmother had celebrated her nine-hundredth naming day before we'd left, and she didn't look like she'd be swimming slowly any time soon.

But humans generally got no longer than a century, and sometimes far less than that.

Although with the look Tessa was giving me, perhaps she'd live longer than I would.

'I'm not going to Aster for help,' she muttered crossly. 'I told him he could take a screencast of Cy and I two nights ago. He sent me an edited version zoomed in on my face. He's not getting *anything* from me until he stops giggling.'

I bit my lip; he'd sent the cast to me, too.

Tessa growled. 'I *am* finding Cy,' she snapped. 'You and Aster can sleep in the pit. Indefinitely.'

With that, she flounced out. I laughed – under my breath, I wasn't stupid – and followed her out, stopping to pull on a shirt.

Cy was in the cockpit, sitting sideways on the pilot's bench, frowning at the wall-sized screen to his side. It showed a schematic for the ship's command system; he didn't seem too upset at the interruption when Tessa swung herself into his lap, especially when he absently stroked her hip and realised that the shirt was *all* she was wearing.

'You smell nice,' he murmured to her. He glanced at me; his eyes were warm. 'Did you have a good swim?'

'Did you know he was in the pool?' she grumbled.

'No. He was supposed to be here. But I suspected otherwise.'

She pouted. I'd shifted into my humanoid form, and the expression had my cock stirring. Cy gave a low chuckle – the sound didn't help my dick – and ran a finger over her lips.

'I like your toes,' he said solemnly.

Tessa gave a terrible imitation of my growl as her body responded to Cy. 'My vagina really *does* have a death wish,' she muttered.

'You are happy with us,' Cy said, then smiled. He studied her carefully, running a diagnostic. 'You need water. And you're sore.'

'I'm *satisfied*,' Tessa countered, which had my chest puffing with pride like a juvenile on its first shark hunt. She thought for a moment. 'And thirsty.'

He settled her next to him. 'Then the bridge is yours. I'll get you a drink.'

I exchanged a grin with Tessa once he'd left; we'd been watching a classic Earth screencast about adventures in space, and Cy had picked up several sayings. Tessa enjoyed it immensely, just as she enjoyed encouraging Cy to talk about what he was feeling, and why he thought it differed from us. She listened to him describe the nuances, and shared screen casts and books when he felt he was floundering. She'd been able to help Cy feel more confident in a handful of weeks than Aster and I had managed over *years*; it was simultaneously galling and made me prouder than I could say.

'Will I ever get used to seeing this?' she murmured, staring out the cockpit glass. She called it *the windscreen* and refused to stop, despite the fact it made me wince.

I dropped a kiss on her head. 'Probably not. I'm starving – can I get you something?'

'Mmm – number four on the breakfast generator, please. *Not* number six, Morgan, or I will dump it in your lap.'

I huffed a laugh and left her to it. *Number six* on the breakfast generator was a concoction of kelp and uncooked sandworms that was an expensive delicacy on Natare; Tessa had paled at the sight of it.

Cy was in the kitchen, fiddling with a body scanner. He didn't need it – his own scanners were equally if not more sophisticated, despite his constant protests that he wasn't supposed to use them like a doctor – but he liked having a second opinion when it came to Tessa, as he was less used to the parameters of her body. There were still parts of it that were a mystery to him – he couldn't see *inside* some of her organs, for instance, which he hated but Tessa was rather pleased about.

I stepped up behind him and bit him gently on the back of the neck, on the spot where I'd almost broken the skin a few nights before. He shivered, then moaned under his breath as I took his hips in my hands and pressed myself against him.

'Didn't Tessa tire you out?' he said breathlessly.

'I could never be too tired for you,' I growled.

He grabbed my hand and kissed it as my fingers wandered towards his crotch. 'Feed your *elyn* first,' he said thickly. He turned to face me, and drew me down for a long, thorough kiss. 'She's waiting. But then come back.'

I pressed the buttons on the generator, and took up the glass of water Cy had already poured from the filter tap.

'Cy, babe,' Tessa called from the pit. 'I thought you said last night that we were the only ship in this sector.'

Cy frowned. 'We should be.'

'Um, well, the radar suggests otherwise.'

The light in the kitchen surged as Aster materialised in the pit, just as the proximity alarm began to blare.

I put the glass in the sink.

'Of all the fucked-up luck,' Aster shouted from the pit. 'Cy! Cloak us, now!'

'What the *fuck*,' I breathed, and sprinted for the cockpit while Cy's eyes clouded as he connected himself with the ship's defence systems.

Tessa had inched over to give Aster space on the pilot's bench; his fingers were flicking furiously over the screen before him.

I took in the radar. 'Oh, *fuck*.' I squeezed Aster's shoulder. 'What the fuck are they doing this far out? Swap.'

Aster completed the sequence on the screen, then moved over, pulling Tessa onto his lap. I ran a series of system checks – the ship was running normally, Cy had raised the sight shield along with the defensive shield, and we had enough oxygen for weeks and ice to last us months – and then killed the engine.

'Morgan?' Tessa said tightly.

'We're just going to coast for a bit, beautiful,' Aster said.

'Coast? Like, just ... float? I thought you said we had to get to Natare as soon as possible because of the peace summit.'

'Mmm-hmm,' Aster agreed. 'I did.'

My fingers paused on the screen; I looked across at Aster. 'You already ...'

'I already,' Aster agreed.

I glanced at Tessa. 'I don't –'

'I knew you wouldn't,' he said softly.

'What are you talking about?' Tessa demanded.

Aster and I studied the screen closely. Aster chewed on his lip.

'Cy!' Tessa called, trying to get up. Aster held her still. 'Cy, they won't tell me –'

'It's the self-destruct sequence,' Aster said grimly, and pulled Tessa closer. 'A code will set off an extra fuse in the engine. It will catch alight immediately, eviscerating the ship and everything on it before you can blink. Immediate, swift death.'

She stared at him. 'Aster. What. The. *Fuck*.' She paused. 'Would you even die?'

'No. But I'd jump into black space once it was done and end myself.'

She put her hands on his biceps and shook him. 'What the *fuck*?'

'A Roth ship.' Cy stood behind us. His expression was rigid. He bent and kissed Aster's hair. 'You did the right thing.'

'Remember what we told you the other week, beautiful?' Aster said lightly. 'That the universe isn't all good? That there are space pirates and unfriendly species and some that are more than unfriendly? The Roth are a warrior race who want to take over their galaxy, and preferably the entire universe. A warrior race who, if they got hold of Morgan, would torture him for information before ransoming him back to his planet for an exorbitant number of credits. They always choose an amount the family can't hope to pay quickly, no matter how rich they are. As an incentive, they transport body parts, accompanied by screencasts of their removal. The Roth are notoriously anti-mechanic, and Cy would fare little better. They wouldn't ask a ransom; they'd just hurt him for fun.' He tipped Tessa's chin up and looked her straight in the eye. 'They'd use you as a breeder. They'd rape you until you fell pregnant, then keep you in a cell until you birthed. I've heard they give the females two days to recover. Then they start it all over again.' His voice shook. 'I'd kill you all myself before I let you go through that. The self-destruct isn't our only option; it's our last line of defence.'

'And that's one of their ships,' she said flatly.

I brought it up on the screen. Our ship was oblong-shaped, with a fat middle and a flattened helm and bow. Roth ships were different, with a rounded, disk-like belly and an extra bit bulging at the front like a head.

'Are they ...' Tessa faltered, staring at the protrusions to the side of the ship's underbelly. 'Does that ship have *legs*?'

'Six of them,' Cy said. His voice was unusually grim. 'It doubles as a terra transport when the Roth ... When they ...'

'When they go hunting,' I finished. 'The ship ... well, it *scuttles*.'

'Like a fucking *spider*?'

'Just like a spider,' Aster answered. 'A spider decorated with antimatter guns and nerve rays.'

Tessa closed her eyes and pushed her face into Aster's shoulder. 'I don't want to know what that means.'

'I hope you never find out,' Cy said softly.

'So we ... coast?'

'For the moment,' I said. 'We're shielded from sight and from their radars, but some of their ships are equipped with infrared systems that will detect light and heat. Our shield is made to conceal our heat signals, but they'll be able to see a blip in the space around us. If we're lucky, they'll think it's junk, or a small asteroid. If we're not ...' I looked across at her. 'Fuck, Tessa, I want you to go and hide. But at the same time, I don't want to let you out of my sight.'

'I'm not going anywhere,' she said.

There was a sharp pang in my chest, and I shifted into my trueform, wrapping them all in limbs. My suckers had flared a wild mix of violent orange and bright red, all but shouting my anxiety.

What a stupid time to realise that I love her, I thought. I risked a sideways glance at Aster, who was looking back at me with a rare expression of compassion. He gave me a tiny nod, like he knew exactly what I was thinking.

I mean, he probably did. I wasn't exactly good at hiding it.

Cy rested his hand on my shoulder and gently squeezed. We coasted silently through space, four pairs of eyes fixed on the radar, barely daring to breathe.

After a handful of minutes, my limbs began to change to a deep, wary pink. I was still on edge, but gradually calming as the Roth ship gave no indication that it had noticed us.

'Don't say it,' Aster said immediately. 'Don't jinx it.'

I frowned. 'Jinx?'

'A human word. To voice a thing will make the opposite thing happen. It brings bad luck. Don't even *think* it.'

'Fine, not thinking it,' I muttered. My limbs tightened on them slightly; Tessa rubbed her cheek against one like an Earth cat.

'Five more minutes,' Cy whispered, as our ship kept coasting. We watched ourselves drift closer to the Roth, the two red blips on the radar a bare hand span apart.

We could see it now, a tiny grey patch in the black outside the cockpit glass.

'Anyone else get the urge to hide?' Aster said, attempting dryness.

'I know they can't see us,' Cy muttered, 'but yes.'

I tensed. My limbs changed colour again, pulsing the brightest red. 'Tessa,' I growled, wanting nothing so much as to bundle her into the bedroom and ensure she was protected, preferably with my body.

'I'm not moving, Morgan.'

The two blips slid slowly closer.

I held my breath.

Aster bit Tessa's shoulder.

'Aster, you dick,' she complained. 'That actually hurt.'

The blips levelled.

Aster covered her shoulder in apologetic kisses and buried his face in her hair, just for a moment.

The blips passed.

I exhaled. My limbs began to fade to a warm pink.

'Fucking *fuck*,' Aster said. 'By the fucking *stars*. Tessa, I hope Morgan didn't wear you out this morning, because –'

'Be quiet, Aster,' Cy hissed.

We all looked up at him in surprise.

He swore. 'Their systems are booting,' he near-shouted. 'Morgan, *go. Go now.*'

I didn't hesitate; my fingers swept over the screen and the gentle, almost-imperceptible rumble of our engine started up again. One of my limbs snaked across Tessa and Aster like a belt.

The ship shot forward and we were pressed back into the seat.

'Cy –' I started.

'They're already on,' Cy said.

I flicked a small orange switch to launch the engine boosters.

Tessa cried out as the ship gained speed, the force pressing her into Aster.

'Hold on,' he whispered to her. 'The environment will stabilise in a few moments. Hold on, starlight.'

She hid her face in his chest and started to count.

She reached twenty before the air pressure and gravity stabilised, and she could peel herself away from Aster, although he didn't let her move far. Her eyes were fixed on the radar, where the two red blips – our ship, and the Roth's – were still concerningly close together.

'It's all right,' Aster said softly. 'They won't touch us.'

The ship lurched.

'Fuck,' I swore.

'They've launched the nets,' Cy confirmed tightly. 'Evade, Morgan.'

'Nets?' Tessa repeated.

'They want to catch us alive, so they won't risk harming the ship and disrupting the life support systems. So ... nets,' I answered, fear crawling up my spine as I tried to fly our ship in ever-changing directions to evade the Roth's sophisticated targeting systems. 'The same type we use to harvest space ice for fresh water. Made of a metal that is both strong and flexible, so it can withstand the pressure of a pulling an object moving at an opposite trajectory – *oh, fuck*.'

The ship lurched again, and my limb was the only thing that stopped Aster and Tessa from spilling onto the floor.

'They've got us,' I said.

Aster tipped Tessa's chin up and gave her a swift, hungry kiss. 'Cy, fasten the shutters.'

The ship whirred. 'Done,' Cy said grimly.

'Morgan, the ... windscreen.'

I flicked back to the cockpit controls and tapped the screen; a moment later, the light dimmed as the glass in the cockpit darkened.

'Just closing your eyes won't be enough,' Aster said warningly, standing up with Tessa in his arms, then setting her back on the chair, her hip pressed to mine.

I swallowed. My stomach was churning; I knew what he was about to do. I reached out and bunched Aster's shirt in my hand. 'I expect you back, starling.'

Aster smirked. 'Yes, Prince.'

Cy grabbed his arms. 'Aster, you *will* come back, won't you? I won't forgive you if you don't.'

Aster kissed Cy gently, then rested his forehead against the cyborg's. 'I know, darling. And you know what to do if I fail. I love you. All of you.'

'Aster, what –' Tessa started, her face stricken with worry and confusion.

Aster glowed briefly, then disappeared.

'Aster!' Tessa yelped.

The radar showed the red blips getting closer; the Roth were visibly reeling us in.

'Come here,' I said. My limbs gathered Tessa up and pulled her into my lap. 'You too, Cy. We have ten seconds.'

Cy slid in next to me. 'Tessa, press your face into Morgan's chest and close your eyes. No matter what you do, don't open them.'

'What –'

'Just do it, starfish,' I whispered.

She buried her face in my chest; I wrapped a limb around her to keep her there, and awkwardly wrapped it around the sides of her face, trying to make sure she could still breathe. Cy's body went limp in an unnervingly lifeless way as he shut down his systems. I covered his eyes with one limb, then flattened another over my own, blocking out the soft glow from the emergency strips completely.

My hearts beat hard in my ears.

A sudden burst of light flared behind my closed eyes, white and bright and blinding. Tessa cried out in pain and surprise; I held her like a vice, not letting her move an inch. My temples throbbed with an instant migraine, a fierce, dull ache settling behind my eyes.

'*Morgan*,' Tessa sobbed, moaning at the pain. 'What the *fuck*.'

'It's all right,' I whispered. 'It's all right, my love. Give it a few more moments, then we'll get you fixed up.'

The light faded gradually, but the pain didn't. Tears were streaming down Tessa's cheeks and straight onto my shirt, but my own weren't any better, dampening Tessa's neck and collarbone.

'Aster did that,' she said thickly after a few moments, finally realising where the light had come from. 'Oh, God, is he all right?'

'He'd better be,' I growled.

'Everyone on that ship –'

'The Roth have a second eyelid to shield their sight from solar rays, but they're only activated as part of their scaled armour. They usually only armour themselves when they're working – or hunting – outside their ships. Without the added protection, their eyes have around the same level of light sensitivity as humans. I would highly doubt there is still a conscious being on that ship.'

'They'll be blinded,' she whispered.

'At least temporarily,' I agreed.

She reached out to the side, her hands groping for Cy. 'Cy? Are you OK?'

'He's out, starfish,' I said, as soothingly as I could manage. 'He turned himself off. Just for a few minutes. He'll reboot, and in the process, any damage done to his eyes will be healed.'

Tessa froze. 'Reboot? But won't that revert his programming back? Will he still ...' She swallowed. 'Will he still know me? Will he still *like* me?'

I snorted. 'Rebooting isn't the same as resetting. If anything, he'll love you more. The feeling won't be a change in his programming; it will be like it's always been there. Don't fret, beautiful. He's rebooted six or so times since I met him. He never once forgot he loved me.'

'Questioned why, once.' Cy's voice came from the side. 'I woke up and he immediately pulled me into the pool. But I didn't forget.'

I forced a chuckle. 'I was worried. Cy, handsome, my eyes aren't ready yet. Can you –'

'On it.' I felt Cy's weight shift, then the sound of his fingers moving across the control screen. The ship made a whirring sound. *'Yes,'* he hissed. 'Aster must have released the nets.'

Tessa pushed against my hold. 'Aster. Where is he?'

'Give him a moment,' I whispered. I forced my eyes open with difficultly; the after-effects were making themselves known in the form of a white ring around my sight and a thumping headache. I nuzzled Tessa's neck, breathing her in, trying to focus. It took a good few blinks before my eyes could make out her curls. 'He would have jumped straight to the nearest star after that. He'll need to feed, then he'll be back. You can open your eyes now, starfish. The light has faded.'

Her eyelids fluttered as she wrenched them open; she gave a small gasp.

'Cy?' I said uneasily. I pulled Tessa to sit straight, cushioning her neck with a limb.

Cy turned, and frowned, and cupped Tessa's cheek with one hand. He gently lifted one of her eyelids, examining her eye.

He swore softly. 'Flash blindness.'

'Temporary,' I asserted.

Cy didn't answer.

'Cy?' I repeated. '*Temporary*?'

Cy's mouth thinned with worry, and my suckers flared a bright, worried scarlet.

TESSA

I COULD ALMOST *FEEL* Morgan and Cy having a silent conversation over my head. 'Cy?' I said shrilly, wishing I could see their
faces. Everything was black. Not the black of night, where you
can still see outlines and see far-away lights, but *pitch* black, as
if all the light in the world had suddenly died. I knew Morgan
was close enough that I should have been able to see the flecks
of sandy-gold in his blue irises; instead, I could see nothing at
all. I blinked rapidly; it made no difference.

'I can't tell,' he said matter-of-factly. 'It's often temporary.
The healing wand should fix it. If you take over here –'

Morgan growled wordlessly. 'Some of the systems are still
down. You'll be able to reboot them faster. Get us out of here,
Cy. The danger hasn't passed yet.' He stood, taking me with
him. I swayed gently in his arms as he carried me from the pit; a
few moments later, I heard the soft sigh of the arched bedroom
door opening, and he settled me down on the bed. 'I'm so sorry,

starfish. I don't want you to be in pain. But I need you and Cy far, far away from that ship, as far as we can possibly get, on the chance that there's another Roth ship somewhere in the system, and Cy will do that faster than I can. Tell me what I can do to help you until Cy has finished.'

'Paracetamol,' I said at once. 'My head is killing me.'

I heard the half-sliding, half-padding sound of him leaving the bedroom. I put my arm across my face, wincing at the blooming pain.

There was a thump next to me, and the bed shifted slightly. 'Well, hello,' Aster crooned. 'Nice of Cy and Mor to prepare me such a lovely reward for my hard work.'

'Aster!' I cried, reaching out blindly towards him. My hand hit something solid – possibly his chest. 'Oh, thank God.'

I felt him sit. 'Tessa, baby, what's wrong?'

'She can't see,' Morgan said shortly, coming back into the room. 'Here, starfish.' He curled the fingers of one hand around two small tablets, and put a glass of water in the other.

'Luckily, I can fix that,' Aster purred.

I swallowed the tablets and drained the glass; it was taken from my fingers. 'What –'

An over-warm hand slid up my thigh. 'You think I would have done that if I couldn't help you, Tessa?'

I swallowed. 'Are the Roth –'

'The ship has stopped. It won't be moving for a while.'

'Are they alive?'

Aster paused. 'I honestly didn't stop to check.'

'Are you all right?'

Aster laughed softly. 'I haven't used so much energy in decades. But I stopped off to eat a star. I hope you three are ready, because I have a lot of excess light to burn.' His fingers slid higher, brushing against my lower lips, tracing upwards before gently rubbing the sides of my clit. My body reacted in an instant, arousal throbbing in my core, despite my headache and the unnerving blankness before my eyes. I could be ninety years old and on my deathbed and Aster could still make me wet. 'Let me fix your headache, then we'll do something about your eyes.'

My breath caught. 'I was hoping Cy would finally probe me. For an abduction, this has been disappointingly light on the probing.'

'Is that so,' Aster said dryly, and slipped a finger inside me. I moaned. 'We can't have *that*. But you have too many clothes on again.'

'I'm not wearing any pants.'

'Mmm,' he agreed. 'I like it. But the shirt needs to go, Tessa. Mor –'

I felt Morgan's gentle hands tug my shirt up; I wriggled, making it easier for him as he pulled it over my head.

'That's better,' Aster purred. His curls brushed my skin as he dropped a line of kisses across my stomach. Another mouth closed over a nipple; it sucked and I felt an answering throb somewhere deep inside me. I whined when it disappeared.

'I'll make sure Cy's got us back on course,' Morgan muttered. He pressed a kiss to my forehead, then I heard him move away.

'Come back quickly,' Aster called after him. 'And put the autopilot on. For at least the next day or so.'

Aster's mouth was always sinful, but he pulled out every trick, nibbling up my thighs and licking my entrance with an obscene sound of enjoyment before turning his attention to my clit; my head throbbed dully, the pain beginning to diminish as my body concentrated on other sensations, every feeling heightened by my lack of sight. He flattened his tongue and worked me with a relentless rhythm, pushing me higher and higher until I couldn't resist any longer and came apart, bunching his hair in my fingers. His tongue slid down and fucked into me through the last throes, lapping at me, making sure I was dripping wet. I'd never been blindfolded before, but after this – after the sheer thrill of putting myself wholly into Aster's hands – I thought it would probably be something I'd request again. Perhaps even often, though preferably without the headache and loss of sight.

'Stars, the *taste* of you,' he said, his voice low and harsh. He reached up to cup my breast, rolling my nipple between his fingers. 'The *sight* of you. You have no idea what you do to me, Tessa.'

I whimpered as he pinched gently, then squirmed.

The pain in my temples had started to lessen, but my sight was still gone, and I wanted to watch when he dragged Morgan and Cy into the bedroom. '*Aster.*'

'You want something, starlight?' he crooned.

'Hurry up and fuck me.'

'Yes, but *where*?' he said, mock-pondering. 'I have a choice to make. Do I slip my cock between your beautiful lips?' He reached up and traced my lips, then dipped a finger into my mouth; I latched onto it immediately, biting down before sucking it up and down until he groaned. 'Or here?' He ran his hand down my body and cupped between my legs, probably drenching his hand in the process. 'Or ...?'
His finger traced my ass, feather-light. I drew in a sharp breath as he collected moisture from elsewhere and drew it down, rubbing it all over me, then gently pushed the tip of his finger inside.

'You want to fuck me there?' I said breathlessly. He hadn't yet, but I'd started to fantasise about what it might feel like, how different it would be to the tip of Morgan's limb.

'I *will* fuck you there,' he said. He withdrew his finger. 'But right now –' he climbed over my body, and dipped his hips against mine, rubbing the head of his erect cock over my entrance '– right now, I think *here.*'

He thrust himself inside me, slamming in to the hilt; I shrieked and arched my back, dragging my nails across his skin. His lips found mine and he kissed me deeply, fucking his tongue into my mouth, keeping time with the thrusts of his hips, grinding down on my clit with every rocking movement. Within moments, I was back on the edge again, so he pulled out slightly, moving quick and shallow, slipping a hand under my ass to angle my hips up so he hit the sweet spot on my inner wall every time.

'Stop messing about,' Morgan growled. I felt him sit on the bed. 'Let her come and heal her eyes, you asshole.'

'I'm going to make you *beg* in five minutes,' Aster promised him. I heard them exchange a kiss above my head without even the slightest stutter to Aster's glorious rhythm.

'Where's Cy?' I gasped.

Lips brushed my forehead. 'Here, Tessa. Always here.'

I groaned as Aster quickened his pace. Fingers slid over my hip and found my clit, gently pinching before pressing down in small circles – Morgan's hand, Morgan's fingers. Aster made a deep, guttural noise, and I suspected that I wasn't the only person Morgan was touching.

My orgasm was sudden and shocking, almost painful in its intensity. My inner muscles clenched around Aster as he thrust deep, and with two more rolls of his hips there was a spurt of heat inside me, spreading out from my core and through my body.

Cy stroked my hair.

My sight didn't return instantaneously, but the remnants of the pain vanished almost immediately.

'Fuck,' I said in surprise. 'You should bottle this, Aster. You'd make a fortune.'

'Go slowly,' Cy whispered, kissing my eyelids when I tried to wrench them open. 'Your body is still remembering the damage. Let her roll over,' he commanded Aster, who slid out of me – still hard, I noticed – and turned me onto my belly.

'Oh, that does *not* help me,' Aster muttered. His hands slid up the backs of my thighs, then cupped my ass.

'This is about her eyes, not your dick,' Morgan snapped. A moment later, he gave a strangled groan – the sound he made when someone had grabbed *his* dick, and things were very much about to become all about it. 'I'm going to fuck you senseless, Aster.'

Aster laughed. It was an oddly sepulchral sound, resonating all the way down to my bones, and nothing at all like his usual laugh. 'I think you've forgotten what I am, little prince,' he purred. 'I let you have your way so often because it pleases me. But I think you might need reminding which one of us is millennia old.'

I rolled slightly to blink fuzzily over my shoulder. Aster's form had grown to be taller than Morgan, his shoulders broader; his arms rippled with muscle as they moved. He was behind Morgan, one hand on Morgan's cock, the other arm crossing his chest. His eyes caught mine over Morgan's shoulder; he winked playfully, the irises glowing gold as he squeezed. The cephalopod gasped, and I watched as Morgan – the always-in-control, possessive, dominant-as-hell Morgan – melted against the body behind him and his head tipped back on Aster's shoulder, completely ceding power.

'Holy shit,' I muttered.

'Indeed,' Cy said breathlessly. He gathered me up and pulled me into his lap, turning me around so I could watch; I could feel his chest rising and falling with his quick, shallow breaths. His cock was rock-hard under my ass and I gently ground against it as Aster's hand began to move. His arm slid back behind Morgan, and the cephalopod made a sound that told me exactly what Aster had started to do.

Cy held my waist with one hand and reached for the lube with the other.

Aster shook his head. 'I don't need it,' he purred. 'Morgan is in heat, aren't you, handsome?'

I blinked and rubbed my eyes gently, wishing things weren't still slightly blurry; I wanted *very* badly to see this. 'He does that?' I murmured to Cy. 'I thought heats were a female thing.'

'Twice a year,' he whispered. 'It's like ... a response to being away from his own kind. It's not supposed to be for another month or so.' He rubbed his cheek on my head. 'Fear might have triggered it to happen sooner.'

'What does it mean?'

Cy snorted. 'It means normal Morgan, only ... more. But with Aster like he is right now, they might keep each other busy for a few days.' He paused. 'I'm glad you're here, Tessa. The last time it happened ... It was a lot.'

I caught his hand and kissed it, silently promising that I'd be there for him. *Especially* when our males were *a lot*.

Which meant every fucking day, *always*.

All three of them hissed as Aster thrust inside Morgan with one hard jerk of his hips. Morgan panted, but his cock stayed hard under Aster's hand, and his expression was one of pleasure, not pain, despite Aster's sudden and intrusive entrance. His eyes rolled back as Aster began to move, so slowly and so thoroughly I imagined I could feel his thrusts myself. I sighed as Cy nuzzled at my neck; I took his hands and wrapped his arms more tightly around me.

'Look at your beautiful mates,' Aster whispered to Morgan, his arm back across Morgan's chest in a tight embrace, almost holding the blonde upright. He dipped his lips to the column of Morgan's throat and sucked, his hips rolling as Morgan moaned. *'Yours*, prince. Do you like knowing that? That they are yours, and you theirs?'

Morgan cried out wordlessly; apparently he *did* like knowing that. Cy's cock twitched beneath me; I instinctively rubbed against it, loving the way he gasped. I reached down and took his thick length in hand and lined it up, then began to sink down on his swollen head, biting my lip at the stretch.

'Tessa, love, you don't have to –' Cy began hoarsely.

'Shh,' I told him, rocking slightly to take his head fully inside. I closed my eyes at the feeling of overwhelming fullness, but I was determined to make Cy feel as good as Morgan was feeling. I kept rocking slightly as I inched further and further down, my progress made slippery by my own slick and by Aster's warm release.

After what felt like years, I stopped sliding, and I realised there wasn't any further to go. I laughed huskily; I felt so full I couldn't take a proper breath. I had the mad urge to high-five myself for a job well done.

'Did it,' I said hoarsely, rocking slightly as Cy's cock rubbed every – and I mean *every* – sweet spot inside me. 'Fucking *finally*. I beat your record, Morgan. I think I deserve a gold star.'

Matching deep groans came from before me; I looked up to see Aster and Morgan's eyes fixed on where Cy was stretching me open.

'Fuck,' Morgan moaned.

'I will bring you every star in the fucking universe,' Aster grated out, his pace quickening.

'I can't look at that,' Morgan said, closing his eyes. 'I'll burst.'

'You're in a heat.' Aster took Morgan's earlobe between his teeth. 'You'll be bursting more than once.'

I turned my head and whispered to Cy; he smiled against my cheek and nodded, brushing his lips down my neck again. He slipped an arm around my waist and we carefully moved forward together, until I was settled on my hands and knees and he was seated deep inside me, my face level with Morgan's cock.

'Fuck,' three voices said at once.

I smiled. I might have been the one on my knees, but they were sweating for *me*, watching my every move, and I wasn't about to pretend that the power of it wasn't intoxicating. I leaned forward; when Aster realised what I wanted, he positioned Morgan so his cock could slip between my lips. I sucked on his head, taking it in my mouth, then backed off, licking the swollen tip, his salty-sweet precum spreading over my tongue.

He tasted like salted caramel.

I slid my mouth over Morgan as Cy began to move with slow, gentle, shallow thrusts, one hand on my hip, the other rubbing up and down my back, almost like he couldn't believe what was happening. Morgan cupped my cheek, his thumb moving back and forth.

'I love you,' he said hoarsely. 'I love you all.'

My heart swelled in my chest.

'We love you, prince,' Aster whispered. 'Now come, darling. This isn't over yet. I'm sure Tessa has something else she'd like to try.'

I flicked my eyes up at him; he grinned, then sank his teeth into Morgan's shoulder, leaving a red mark.

Oh.

Somehow, Aster knew what I wanted, what I was desperate to have. My eyes blurred at his ability to seemingly read my mind, and I doubled my efforts on Morgan's cock, licking and sucking and swirling my tongue as Cy's hips quickened.

Morgan's hand bunched in my hair and his cock twitched and thickened before my mouth flooded with his cool jellied cum. I swallowed, my throat working furiously to manage how *much* there was. I tried not to drool; it really was fucking delicious, and my saliva glands apparently thought so too.

Aster made a rasping sound as he came with a single deep thrust into Morgan. His form shrank slightly, back to his usual size, though his eyes stayed abnormally bright. He slid slowly from Morgan.

Morgan spun to grab his bicep. 'Not outside,' he said hoarsely. 'Don't you dare leave again.'

Aster kissed him tenderly. 'I won't go outside. I promise.' He glowed darkly for a moment before disappearing; a moment later, I heard the bathroom door close so he could clean up the organic way.

Morgan surged forward and pulled me away from Cy, kissing me furiously, apparently uncaring that my mouth tasted like him. His hands slid to my ass, squeezing and kneading in a way that made my entire body clench. Cy knelt behind me, his cock rock-hard against my back, his hands cupping my breasts, rolling and pulling and pinching my nipples until I was shaking.

Aster walked back in, his raven-black hair slicked back from his face. His cock was still hard; he reached down to stroke it when he saw us.

My eyes were almost back to normal, and just seeing them all made me bite back a moan. Morgan dragged my face to his and thrust his tongue into my mouth; a moment later, he'd shifted forms, and limbs were winding up my legs.

'That's better,' Aster purred. He prowled to the side of the bed and seized Cy's mouth with his, stroking Cy's cheek and neck with gentle fingers. He whispered something in Cy's ear, something that made the cyborg groan, and they swapped places, Aster slipping behind me to take me in his arms, Cy kneeling behind Morgan, nipping the back of his neck.

'I could watch you forever,' I said breathlessly.

'Just watch?' Cy murmured.

'No,' I said truthfully, as Aster sucked hard enough on my neck to leave a bruise. 'No. Not just watch. I need to touch.'

Aster ran his hand down my spine. 'I don't believe in gods, starlight, but I've never felt so blessed.'

I lifted my hand and ran my fingers through his hair. 'You fucking romantic.'

He snorted and slapped my ass, then dipped his fingers between my legs. 'You know what I want to do to you?'

I shivered. 'Yes.'

'Do you want to?'

I took a deep breath. 'Yes.'

'So much as a wince and I'll stop,' he promised. 'You just have to tell me, Tessa.'

I turned my face so I could bite his bottom lip. 'I know, Aster. I trust you.'

'I love you,' he mouthed against my lips. 'You impossible, clever, beautiful thing.'

If he hadn't been holding me up, I would have melted into a puddle right there.

His fingers traced a circle around my ass, teasing. It only made me wetter, more eager. He rubbed his cock between my legs, soaking it, then pressed a finger inside me. I exhaled and tried to relax, tried not to give in to the instinct to tense, and he moved it back and forth until I was used to the movement. The lube that Cy had grabbed was still on the bed, and I heard him open it one handed; he withdrew his finger, and slid it back in a moment later, slick with lubricant and with a friend. The two fingers stretched me pleasantly, much like Morgan's limb had. I moaned.

Aster nibbled my neck. 'Make yourself useful, Morgan,' he commanded, and Morgan dipped his face to take my nipple in his mouth, his tongue curling around the aching tip before he sucked hard enough to make me squeak. Aster gently fucked me with his fingers, then withdrew again; then it wasn't his fingers fucking me.

I let my head loll back as he pushed his cock inside me. He wasn't his usual size, but as he moved in and out, making sure to keep me slippery with a mixture of my own arousal and lube, I felt him swell slowly and carefully until he was filling me.

He kissed my shoulder. 'All right?'

He rolled his hips; I hissed in pleasure. 'Better than all right.'

'We're going to go backwards,' he said softly. 'I've got you.'

He sank back on the pillows, taking me with him. His hand made its way across my belly and down, cupping between my legs, sinking a finger inside me and pressing the heel of his hand on my clit. 'Tessa?'

'Don't stop,' I moaned.

He immediately stopped, huffing a laugh. 'I think she's ready for you, princeling.'

Morgan's eyes were dark with want as he surged over me, kissing Aster fiercely before seizing my mouth. 'In or out?'

'In,' I begged. 'Hurry up, Morgan.'

Limbs snaked out to part my legs, holding my knees wide apart. It made Aster shift more deeply inside me; I whimpered, but Aster readjusted, soothing me, moving shallowly and then stopping when Morgan pushed two fingers inside me.

'Oh, stars, I can feel that,' Aster said breathlessly. 'Cy, please tell me you're ready.'

'Please tell me you're not,' Cy muttered.

I laughed. Morgan angled down so I could wrap my arms around his neck. 'After this, it's Cy's turn to be spoiled. For *hours*.'

Morgan's mating shaft stroked around where Aster was buried inside me, then moved forward, tracing my swollen lips and pushing its tip inside my entrance. I threw my head back, panting his name as he pushed further in; behind me, Aster swore. Cy had made me more than ready, and Morgan hissed my name as his shaft pushed in as far as it could go.

I couldn't move. I whimpered, shuddering, feeling so full I could barely draw breath. Aster and Morgan froze as I tried to overcome the notion that I was pinned in place.

'Tessa, baby, relax,' Aster crooned.

'I need to move,' I panted. 'Aster, I need to come.'

He nuzzled my ear. 'Then let us make you.'

Morgan began to move gently, a limb snaking between our bodies to rest its fluttering suckers directly on my clit. When he pulled back, Aster pushed in, and the two of them moved in an alternating rhythm that had me sweating at the overpowering feeling of fullness.

'Cy,' Aster said warningly.

Cy kissed his way down Morgan's spine; I couldn't see where he stopped, and made a mental note to request he do that another time, when I could watch. A moment later, his mouth was back on Morgan's neck, and Morgan let his head drop onto my breast, moaning as Cy worked his way inside his body. Morgan stilled completely, so that every movement Cy made caused one inside me; it might have been Morgan stretching me, but it was Cy doing the fucking.

I wrapped my arms around Morgan and tentatively raised my knees.

Morgan and Aster groaned in unison, the movement shifting them in me – and against each other, separated by some thin wall of muscle. They pushed up against each other inside me; Morgan's limb latched onto my clit and *sucked*.

Both thrust deep, filling me up, stretching me. I felt so full I wanted to scream but I came instead, tears running down my cheeks as my body squeezed them both. My eyes fluttered closed and I saw stars as my knees gripped Morgan's sides. He gave three quick, shallow thrusts, then buried himself deeply inside me as he came, calling my name. His head dropped again and he kissed a line down my exposed throat.

Pain shot through me as his teeth pierced my skin where my neck met my shoulder.

A moment later, suckers were tracing over the wound, leaving behind a cool smear of lubricant – or possibly cum. I didn't much care as it stopped the pain immediately, leaving behind a shiver of pleasure lacing from the bite straight to my core. My body clenched around Morgan's shaft in the swiftest, gentlest orgasm I'd ever had, my body almost floating on the waves of feeling, waves that rolled for moments or minutes or maybe even lifetimes as I whimpered, swept away by the overwhelming sensation.

Morgan and Aster groaned.

'Beautiful,' Cy said breathlessly.

'Morgan,' I groaned. 'Morgan, I can feel –'

'I know,' he murmured, brushing a tear from my cheek. 'I know.'

Because I could *feel* him through the bite. It simmered just beneath my own conscious thought, like a deep well had opened up within some secret part of me, a part I'd never known existed. New feelings spilled from it, feelings that weren't *mine*: I could feel Morgan's pride and his awe and his *love*. My heart swelled almost painfully; my eyes stung with tears again as he kissed me tenderly.

'Mine,' I whispered.

'Yours,' he agreed.

'*Ours*,' Aster said, and wrenched Morgan forward, kissing him fiercely. Cy made a hoarse, wordless sound, which Morgan echoed; Aster turned my face to suck on my bottom lip, giving two swift thrusts and filling me with warmth. He pulled back slightly. 'Bite,' he demanded, baring his neck.

When Morgan sank his teeth into Aster's neck, I swore, overwhelmed. It was Aster's *power* I felt first, the immense searing heat of it, and his age. It settled alongside Morgan's deep, still well of emotion, and immediately made me crave a star-filled sky. 'Fuck, Aster,' I said thickly. 'You're *ancient*.'

'I'm young for my kind,' he protested. 'In fact, I'm younger than you, in equivalence.'

'No wonder you act it.'

He grinned, then pulled me in for a kiss, flexing his hips until I gasped. 'Never leave us.'

Morgan's mating shaft slipped from inside me as Cy began to fuck him in earnest, working in a relentless rhythm that had Morgan rasping his name over and over in senseless praise. Aster groaned, watching them, and gently repositioned me on my knees, holding me up as he gently moved inside me, the fingers of his spare hand moving to fill where Morgan had left empty, the heel of his hand pressing down on my clit.

I came again, sobbing, and took him with me. His heat radiated through me as he grated out my name, and a moment later my sight was back to normal and the slight soreness between my legs had disappeared. When I came back to myself, he gently pulled out of my body.

'Look at them,' he whispered in my ear, wrapping his arms around me. 'Look at them watching you.'

He was right; both Cy and Morgan were watching us. Cy's grey eyes were wild with want, and Morgan's face was dewy with sweat. I'd never seen anything so beautiful, and I let Aster spread my knees and reach down to toy with my overly-sensitive flesh and the mess seeping out of me onto the bedspread.

Cy and Morgan gave matching moans. Cy's eyes fluttered closed as he came; his hand reached around to grip Morgan's mating shaft, and Morgan shouted as jelly seeped in pulses from his suckers all over the bed. Cy withdrew, and fell forward to lie face-down, panting in a rare show of exertion. I reached over and stroked his cropped auburn hair.

Morgan leaned over almost lazily, and bit him on the back of the neck. When I felt Cy, I all but swooned, like some Victorian lady; Aster had to hold me upright as I sorted through his complexity and sweetness.

It was as if they were somehow below my skin, thrumming with my heartbeat, part of my body as well as my mind. They were so distinct, their core emotions – the bits that made them wholly themselves, and no other – snaking through the very essence of me, twining with the things *I* was, balancing out in harmony.

It was *perfect*.

'That's different,' I managed.

Cy nodded. He shifted on the bed, looking up at us, his expression flickering between consternation and joy. I stroked his cheek.

'It's the same,' I breathed to him. 'What you feel. The love. Cy, it's the *same*.'

'I –' he started, his voice thick with emotion. He shook his head, then rubbed his cheek on my hand. 'How the fuck can Aster still be horny?'

I snorted and stretched. 'He can help himself out with that. I'm exhausted.' I reached up to touch my bite, smiling slightly.

Then sat upright when I couldn't feel the raised scar.

'Mirror,' I said to the wall; the featureless beige shifted into a reflection of the four of us on the bed, my eyes wide and my hair wild.

I rubbed the blood off my neck. There was nothing underneath it.

'No.' I stared at my reflection. My neck was as it had been that morning. *'Aster!'*

'Please tell me you're ready again,' Aster purred, kissing up my back.

'You asshole! You healed my bite!'

He stilled, then swept my hair aside to examine my collar-bone. 'Oh, *fuck*.'

I watched his muscles bunch in the mirror. 'You're lucky you're pretty, Aster,' I snarled. Tears burned in my eyes. I reached up to angrily wipe them away.

'We'll put them back,' he said. 'Morgan can bite you a second time, and then I'll ...' He swallowed. 'I just won't come inside you again.'

I stared at his face in the mirror. He was entirely serious. 'You won't ... *Ever*?'

'No,' he said, determined. 'If you want the bite, then that's what you'll have.'

'That will work until the first time Tessa gets a cold,' Morgan said.

'There are doctors on your planet, fish-brain,' Aster sniped.

Morgan snorted. 'Yes, like you'll let Tessa wait to see a doctor when you could heal her in two minutes.'

Cy took my hand. 'Can you still feel us, Tessa?'

I frowned, then closed my eyes. I breathed in, trying to con-centrate. At first, I could only feel worry, but then I realised it wasn't all mine. Cy was concerned, Morgan was desperate to make me happy, and Aster was riding a giant wave of guilt.

'I can feel you,' I said. I exhaled, and opened my eyes to frown at myself in the mirror.

'Then why aren't you happier?' Cy said softly.

I took them all in. Aster's raven hair and golden skin next to Morgan's blonde waves and deep tan, with Cy and his red-haired, fair beauty behind. Cy and Aster with bites on their necks, proclaiming that they were claimed, taken, *loved*, and Morgan's sharp fangs that showed immediately exactly who it was that loved them.

Aster blinked at me in the mirror. 'Ah,' he said, then his face cleared. He glowed, and disappeared.

A moment later, he was walking back into the bedroom, still stark naked but holding something in one hand. 'It's a symbol, isn't it?' he said gently. 'Something that announces an attachment the moment you see it. It tells other beings that you *belong*, doesn't it, starlight? That we want you; that we *chose* you. That you're ours and we're yours.'

'Oh, Tessa,' Cy said softly. 'You don't need a bite to make that true.'

Morgan was watching Aster. He frowned, then blinked. 'Ah.' He smiled, a wide grin that made him breathtakingly beautiful. 'Good thinking, my love.'

'A bite isn't the only thing that can do that,' Aster said to me gently. 'The bite is about the connection, and you have that now. But you should have something else, too.' He knelt before me. It should have looked silly – he was completely naked and still half-hard – but it was magnificent instead. I ran my hands over his broad shoulders. He caught my left hand, and pushed something cool and hard over my ring finger.

'I started making this three years ago,' he went on softly, 'when we started researching human customs and what you might expect, what might make you happy. But I only finished it a handful of weeks ago. When I met you at Advena, Morgan and Cy were buying the finishing touch.' He lifted my hand.

The ring was made of three slender bands, one gold, one silver, and one black, interlocking elegantly beneath a simple square claw which held a diamond larger than my fingernail.

'Fuck,' I said stupidly.

'It's perfect, Aster,' Morgan said thickly.

'When we asked you what *fifteen point ninety K* meant, we could tell that you knew,' Aster went on. 'And so I Googled it. I have to say that humans really nailed that search engine. It came up on the first page.'

I stared at the ring.

'I don't believe in gods, but when I found out it was a ring size, and a ring size you recognised *immediately*, and I was already making a ring, well ...' He gave a half-shrug. 'I might start praying again.' He bent and kissed me softly. 'We didn't think you'd want to do this, Tessa. We didn't think you'd just ... accept us. Want to be with us in the way we craved, even if you came with us. Even if you loved us. We thought it was impossible. We thought *you* were impossible. Instead, you're more than we ever dreamed.' Aster lifted my hand to his mouth and brushed his lips across my knuckles. 'So you can wear this if you want, as a symbol. Something to tell others that you belong. That you're ours and we're yours.'

'You *made* it?' I said, my voice wavering. 'You made it yourself?'

'I *did* tell you that I'd done some metalwork. I managed rather well, didn't I?' he said admiringly. 'It was my first time, but I think I'll get better with more practice.'

'More practice?'

'If you can't have a bite, then I'm going to drape you in gold,' he purred. 'And then Tirian rose platinum, which is worth *far* more.'

I fell back on the bed, raising my hand to admire the ring. It was gorgeous, something I never would have picked for myself, but somehow perfectly *right*. It was the ring I'd once been so desperate for – but Cy was right, I realised. I *didn't* need it. I *was* wanted. I *was* loved. I *did* belong – ring or no ring. But knowing they'd planned for this, that Aster had spent time working on the design, and had shaped it with his own hands – that meant *everything*. I cleared my throat. 'Black for you, gold for Morgan, silver for Cy.'

'And the diamond for you, to balance it,' Aster said. 'That's what Cy and Morgan were buying while I was grinding against you on the Advena dance floor. The stone is conflict-free, by the way. Cy kept the certification. I watched a screencast on it, and it seemed important. We could have gotten a stone from elsewhere in the universe, but we thought you might like to always have a tiny piece of the Earth close by, if you did decide to come with us.'

'It's stunning. I can't stop looking at it.'

'Then don't.' Aster lifted my head so I was pillowed on his chest. Morgan stretched alongside me, taking a lock of my hair in his fingers. Cy snuggled against my other side, his cheek on my belly.

I sighed, warm and content, and turned my cheek to the mirror. Aster let his head drop over the edge of the bed and grinned at me, upside-down. A limb rippling with shades of green and blue slid over my hip to keep me close, its suckers fluttering against my bare skin in a constant caress. Cy nuzzled my stomach, then reached up to twine his fingers through mine.

I smiled back at Aster, and let my hand fall, the ring an unfamiliar weight on my finger. It was beautiful, and it was right, but it wasn't the most beautiful thing in the room, nor the most perfect.

'I still don't really know how to be your *elyn*,' I said.

Aster blinked. 'Just stand still and we'll move around you,' he said, echoing what I'd told him on the dance floor of Advena, all those weeks ago. 'You're not just our *elyn*, Tessa. You're our sun.'

EPILOGUE

TESSA

Natare looked a lot like Earth.

It wasn't exact, of course. The Earth was just over seventy percent water, and Natare was closer to ninety. The land masses were tiny but constant, like the ocean was interrupted by little pinpoints of islands, unlike the Earth's sizable continents.

The water was different, too, much of it blue-green rather than the sharp blue I was used to. Morgan said it was because of the kelp forests beneath the surface; they made the light refract differently. The planet had one sun, like Earth, but it had three moons. Some Enterocti prayed to them, leaving offerings when they were full. Morgan said it was a throwback to ancient times; the people knew the moons weren't gods, but they liked the ritual and the calmness of prayer.

'Ready not-ready?' Cy whispered, resting his chin on my shoulder and slipping his arms around my waist.

'Ready not-ready,' I agreed.

He drew my arm up and used it to point towards an island that was slightly larger than most. 'That's the Capitol.' He shifted our hands across, finding another tiny island. 'And the summer nest is there.'

I tapped my foot nervously. 'I'm going to miss Morgan when we go to the nest.'

'We all will, but don't tell *him* that,' Aster said, standing beside me and handing me a cup of coffee.

I rose on my toes and kissed his cheek. 'Thank you.'

'And don't tell him *that,* either,' he said under his breath, nodding to the mug.

I sipped it. He'd made it perfectly. 'I'm not stupid, Aster.'

He kissed Cy over the top of my head, then rubbed his cheek on my hair. 'How are you feeling?'

'Like I would sell you to space pirates for a family block of peppermint chocolate,' I growled.

'It'll be the first thing I program into the generator,' Cy promised.

'Lucky Mor will be in the Capitol. He wouldn't let you eat *that*, either.'

'Yes, but apparently there's a double standard for raw fish,' I said grumpily. 'He insists sashimi is necessary for growing bone structures, but apparently caffeine is the devil.' I took a mouthful of the awful instant coffee I'd taken with me – of the *one cup* I was allowed per day – defiantly.

'You were the one who left that book open on your tablet,' Aster said mildly. 'He would never have known otherwise.'

I glared at him. 'Now I'd sell you for a *snack-sized bar* of peppermint chocolate. Maybe even a single *piece*.'

'Then who'd take your side against Morgan?'

'Cy would,' I said immediately

'Me,' Cy protested at the same time.

'Fine, fine,' Aster said, grinning. 'You can sell me to space pirates for a single piece of peppermint chocolate.'

'I want that in writing,' I told him.

He bent and kissed my belly. 'I'll give you anything you want, starlight.'

For four smart beings, we'd been pretty stupid. When Cy had used his healing wand – still not, to my eternal disappointment, a probe – to dissolve my IUD and build tiny organic blockers in my fallopian tubes to prevent pregnancy, I'd been looking forward to enjoying life without the headaches and the general moodiness I'd grown used to with hormonal contraception. Cy had been happy to solve a problem in a way that was painless and non-invasive, and Morgan and Aster were as overjoyed as any human man would have been at the prospect of coming inside me with impunity.

Except – fools that we were – we overlooked Aster. Or, more specifically, his organic material that healed me – including the bits of me that weren't broken and I quite wanted to stay.

I'd taken to calling it super spunk, which Aster thought was hilarious.

Less funny, of course, when you feel a weird twinge in your stomach one day, and start vomiting the next, and five days later your cyborg boyfriend scans your womb and finds there's something *living* in it.

You have a choice, Tessa, he'd said, his perfect face blankly serious. *This is your decision to make, and I'll help you either way. If you want, this can stay between us.*

I'll think about it, I'd answered, and I had –

For all of ten minutes.

I hadn't needed that long – I'd settled on my answer almost immediately – but I waited a while longer to make it seem like I'd actually considered the choice Cy was giving me. I loved that he'd asked, that he would have kept it a secret if I'd wanted – but when I put my hand on my belly, I found that I didn't want to do that.

I'd tried to wait before I said anything, but Morgan had opened my tablet to find the pregnancy book I'd been reading, he'd come to me alone and given me the same choice Cy had, his expression an odd, enthralling mix of shock and hope and worry. *I'll help you with whatever you want. With whatever you need.*

It's okay, I'd said. *I want this.*

Aster, the one who'd *caused* the problem, was entirely oblivious until he finally noticed that I dashed to the bathroom the moment I woke up three days in a row. Even then, it was only when I refused a cup of tea, gagging at the smell of the long-life milk, that he put it all together. He'd literally started *glowing* with happiness, dampened only when he anxiously rubbed my back as I heaved into the toilet.

We didn't know which of them was the biological father. *I didn't expect a pregnancy,* Cy said dryly when Morgan demanded an image; *I seem to have left my ultrasound scanner at home. Also, I'm not actually a doctor.* Cy's scanners couldn't see clearly enough through the amniotic fluid to make out a form, but he could hear that there were two heartbeats. He didn't know whether that meant there was *one* baby Enterocti with two hearts, like Morgan had, or *two* human-ish babies with a starling father. Cy thought that an Enterocti was more likely, given that Morgan and I were genetically similar, but Aster said that his kind had bred successfully with other species before, and it was just as likely to be him.

I think he secretly wanted it, even more than Morgan did.

I worried almost constantly about what the baby – or babies – might look like, and what *birth* might be like, but Cy said calmly that if the species traits hadn't meshed, the new life probably wouldn't have survived. The pregnancy seemed to be progressing more or less in line with normal human gestation, which Cy said might indicate that human traits might be equal, if not dominant. I couldn't help imagining tiny baby starlings that might float to the ceiling in sleep – or in mischief – or a miniature Morgan who discovered they could camouflage and grab eight different sharp things at once.

They'll have three fathers, starlight, Aster pointed out. *If they fly up, I'll bring them down. If they swim, Morgan will swim after them.* He'd paused. *And, if by some miracle they're Cy's, then he'll teach them how to feel.*

'Tessa,' Morgan growled from behind us. 'I can *smell* that coffee.'

'I can have one cup, Morgan,' I growled straight back.

'The book said –'

'Keep talking, babe, and you'll be sleeping on the floor tonight.'

Morgan closed his mouth.

I sipped my coffee smugly.

'He's just nervous about seeing his mother,' Aster said airily.

'So are you,' Morgan shot back.

'Of course I am,' Aster said. 'Your mother is terrifying.'

I winced.

Cy squeezed my hips gently. 'She'll love you, Tessa.'

'She'll *adore* you,' Morgan agreed, coming to stand at my other side. He took my coffee cup, and then my hand, and together we stared down at his planet.

My new home.

Cy made a contented sound. 'What made you decide to come with us in the end?' he asked me softly. 'You never told us.'

I looked at our reflection in the glass. Morgan to one side, Aster to the other, with Cy standing behind, and me in the middle. I caught Aster's eyes and smiled.

'The view.'

THE END

Advena Abductions will continue with Maeve's story, *INTO ORBIT*.

Also by Hollie Hartwright

The Advena Abductions Series
Book One: Count Down
Book Two: Into Orbit
Book Three: Dark Space
Book Four: Safe Landing

www.ingramcontent.com/pod-product-compliance
Lightning Source LLC
Chambersburg PA
CBHW030629120726
47904CB00006B/2091